THOROUGHBRED

ARABIAN CHALLENGE

CREATED BY
JOANNA CAMPBELL

WRITTEN BY
KAREN BENTLEY

HarperPaperbacks
A Division of HarperCollinsPublishers

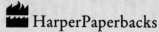

HarperPaperbacks
A Division of HarperCollins*Publishers*
10 East 53rd Street, New York, N.Y. 10022-5299

This is a work of fiction. The characters, incidents, and dialogues are products of the author's imagination and are not to be construed as real. Any resemblance to actual events or persons, living or dead, is entirely coincidental.

Copyright © 1997 by Daniel Weiss Associates, Inc. and Joanna Campbell

ISBN 0-06-106492-0

Cover art: © 1997 Daniel Weiss Associates, Inc.

First printing: August 1997

Printed in the United States of America

Visit HarperPaperbacks on the World Wide Web at
http://www.harpercollins.com

❖ 10 9 8

TO JOHN

1

CINDY McLEAN STEADIED HER HANDS ON BLACK REASON'S neck, adjusted her balance in the saddle, and looked straight ahead between the beautiful Thoroughbred colt's ears at the metal bars of the starting gate. "Steady, boy," she murmured. "This is our big chance." In seconds the starter at the Gulfstream Park track would flip open the gate. If Cindy could stay in the saddle and ride well, she would be cleared for her apprentice jockey's license—and given permission to ride in a real race.

I've wanted to be a jockey for so long, Cindy thought. *Now I'm almost sixteen and finally old enough to ride on the track. I'm really about to do this.*

1

Black Reason's ears tipped back, then pricked again. He stood as still as a statue, awaiting the familiar sound of the starting bell. Black Reason was bought at the Churchill Downs horses-in-training sale the last summer, and he had come a long way. Cindy had been his exercise-rider from the day the sleek, three-year-old black colt had stepped from the van at Whitebrook, the Thoroughbred breeding and training farm near Lexington, Kentucky, where Cindy lived. Last fall Black Reason had won an allowance race at Belmont and a minor stakes at Churchill Downs with Ashleigh Griffen riding.

Ashleigh's the best jockey there is, Cindy thought. *I want to ride just as well as she does.*

Cindy crouched forward slightly. She felt tense but confident, and every bit of her attention was focused on her horse and the stretch of track ahead of them.

The bell shrilled, sounding much louder in Cindy's ears than it did from the grandstands. "Go!" Cindy cried, kneading her hands along the colt's neck to ask for speed.

Black Reason leaped out of the gate into a full racing gallop. His muscles bunched powerfully under his satiny black coat as his hooves dug into the soft, harrowed surface of the track. Cindy went with him easily, balancing over the colt's withers in the tiny racing saddle.

Once they were clear of the gate Cindy guided

Black Reason toward the inside rail. The colt settled instantly into his trademark long, steady strides, hugging the rail.

"That's it!" Cindy cried, breathless. "You're doing great, boy!"

Black Reason flicked back his ears, awaiting instructions. Cindy let him gallop out another furlong before slowing him to a trot. Laughing with pride and relief, she turned him back toward the starting gate.

Cindy prayed that she had passed her test. She thought that her ride had been nearly flawless. "Thanks, Reason," she whispered, stroking the colt's jet-black neck.

Black Reason huffed out a grateful sigh at her words and continued on at a level trot, doing exactly what she asked. He wasn't a grandstander like Champion, Cindy thought. Wonder's Champion, last year's Triple Crown winner and a colt Cindy had helped train, always seemed to know when he had done well. Champion would have been acting up by now, prancing and tossing his head as he tried to get as much praise and attention as possible. Black Reason was obedient and game but much gentler. He looked to Cindy for direction about how he should act.

"Champion may grab all the headlines, but I love you, too," Cindy said to the black colt. "You always try so hard."

This year is starting out to be a great one, she thought happily. Recently Champion had been invited to race in the exclusive Dubai World Cup in the United Arab Emirates at the end of March. There he would take on the best horses in the world. Cindy would be traveling to the United Arab Emirates, too, as Champion's groom.

Waiting at the gap with the starter were Ashleigh and Mike Reese, Ashleigh's husband and co-owner of Whitebrook. Cindy's family was also there.

Cindy stopped Black Reason at the gap and looked at the starter, her heart pounding in her chest. She couldn't tell from his face what he thought of her ride. *What if I didn't pass?* she worried. *Maybe I made a mistake somewhere that I don't know about.*

The starter made a note on a clipboard. "Well done," he said. "Here's your okay card. You can ride in a race now."

Cindy let out her breath in relief. "Thank you so much!" She could feel the tension draining out of her shoulders and back. *I'm glad that's over!* she said to herself. *If I had failed, I would have been devastated.*

Cindy knew she still had one more major test to pass—in her first race the steward would be watching her closely to see if she could handle her mount under real racing conditions. *But hopefully the race will go as well as my gate test,* she thought.

"Excellent ride, Cindy," said Samantha McLean,

Cindy's redheaded adoptive sister. Samantha looked pleased for her but a little wistful. Cindy's older sister was involved with every aspect of training at Whitebrook and had trained her Thoroughbred mare Shining into a champion. But at twenty-one, Samantha was five-foot five and weighed a hundred and twenty-five pounds. She was too tall and heavy to be a jockey. Cindy was happy she seemed to have stopped growing at five foot three, like Ashleigh had.

"That was a nice ride, sweetheart," acknowledged Ian McLean, Cindy's adoptive father. Ian was head trainer at Whitebrook.

Cindy laughed. "Don't look so worried, Dad."

"I am worried," Ian said, frowning. "I'm pleased you did so well. But this means you'll be riding in races, and that's a lot different from exercise-riding. It's much more dangerous—especially if you're inexperienced."

"No doubt about that," Mike agreed. Ashleigh's handsome blond husband was also an excellent trainer.

"I know," Cindy said patiently. But she was sure that she was born to ride in races. Since Ian and Beth had adopted her four years ago, Cindy had ridden one of Whitebrook's many majestic, high-strung Thoroughbreds almost every day. Usually she rode one of her favorites—March to Glory, the gray stallion she had exercise-ridden and helped train to Horse of the Year honors two years ago; Champion, a difficult but supremely talented colt; and now Honor Bright, the youngest granddaughter of Ashleigh's Wonder, Ashleigh's miracle race mare. Honor had gone into training last fall.

"Cindy's always careful when she rides," put in Beth McLean, Cindy's adoptive mother. She was holding Kevin, Cindy's two-year-old brother. Green eyed and redheaded, Kevin looked much like Samantha.

"Thanks, Mom." Cindy looked quickly at Ashleigh to see what she thought of her ride. Cindy appreciated her family's support, and she was glad they were proud of her. But Ashleigh's approval meant more to her than anyone's.

Cindy had looked up to Ashleigh ever since she had met her. Star jockey and trainer, Ashleigh had trained Wonder and had ridden her to victory in the Breeders' Cup Classic and had ridden Wonder's oldest son, Wonder's Pride, to wins in the Kentucky Derby and Classic. Last spring and summer Ashleigh had been Champion's jockey in his three Triple Crown race victories. Cindy could hardly wait to hear what Ashleigh thought of her ride today.

"Good job, Cindy." Ashleigh's hazel eyes were smiling. "I couldn't have done better."

Cindy's heart filled with pride. Ashleigh was a kind person, but Cindy knew she would never compliment anyone just to flatter them.

Ashleigh set down Christina, her three-year-old daughter, careful to move her away from Black Reason's hooves. "Go to Daddy," she said, pointing at Mike.

Cindy noticed with amusement that Christina turned right around and headed for Black Reason. Small as she was, Christina already loved horses.

Black Reason dropped his head almost to the ground to look at the little girl and sniffed. He seemed to want to meet Christina as much as she wanted to meet him. "Nice horse," Christina pronounced. "Go for a ride."

Ashleigh scooped up her daughter. "No, you're not going to ride the horses here at the track." Ashleigh looked back at Cindy. "But I hope you are," she added. "How would you like to ride Black Reason in his first start of the year?"

"I'd love to!" Cindy had dreamed that Ashleigh would ask her that. Cindy imagined herself riding confidently in an actual race, wearing the blue-and-white silks of Whitebrook, just the way Ashleigh did. "I can't wait!" she added.

"I'll pick a race for him in a couple of weeks here at Gulfstream," Ashleigh said. "How does that sound?"

"Fantastic!" Cindy knew she was grinning from ear to ear. *I can't believe this is all really happening*, she thought, turning to lead Black Reason back to the barn to cool him out. *Sometimes my life is just too good to be true!*

"We've got plans to make for the other horses, too," Mike said. "How do you think Limitless is looking, Ian?"

Cindy stopped for a second to listen. She knew they were talking about Limitless Time, the bay four-year-old son of Fleet Goddess. Fleet Goddess had been Ashleigh's next superstar race mare, after Wonder.

Limitless had worked earlier that morning on the track. Four Whitebrook horses were in Florida at Gulfstream for the winter races—Champion, Black Reason, Limitless, and Blue Note, a three-year-old allowance horse. They had all spent most of the winter at a nearby training farm.

"Limitless definitely improved as a three-year-old," Ian said.

Limitless had won stakes races at Saratoga in the summer and Belmont in the fall. *Limitless really can close,* Cindy thought, remembering the bay colt's dramatic come-from-behind finishes.

"Cindy, we're going out to the training farm in a little while," Samantha called after her.

Cindy stopped and turned back to the group. "We're bringing the other horses to the track today, right?"

"Yes, we'll leave as soon as you get Black Reason settled," Ian said.

As she headed toward the barn Cindy's pulse quickened with excitement at the thought of the horses' return. She knew that meant the start of their spring campaigns, especially Champion's on the road to the Dubai World Cup. *That's going to be such an incredible race,* she thought. *Talk about competition!*

Back at the barn Cindy draped a sheet over Black Reason and walked the colt around the stable yard until his coat was dry. As she walked she replayed her ride over and over in her mind.

"I'm a real jockey, boy," she said to Black Reason as she put the colt in crossties to brush him. "So this is how a real jockey feels and acts!" Cindy cocked her head thoughtfully, holding a currycomb in midair. "I don't feel that different, though. I wonder if I should?"

Black Reason huffed out a sigh and dropped his head. He seemed to wish she would just hurry up and brush him.

Cindy laughed. "Okay, I'll get going. I know that even though I'm a jockey now, I still have to do my chores."

She brushed Black Reason until the colt's coat glittered like black diamonds. Then she packed his brushes in his tack trunk and stepped away from the stall.

"Now what should I do?" she asked herself. "What would a really great jockey like Ashleigh do?"

Black Reason put his head over the netting on his door. He nudged her fondly, but he didn't seem to have any suggestions.

"Maybe I don't feel different after my ride this morning because I'm not on Ashleigh's level as a jockey," Cindy said, patting the colt's nose. "After all, I haven't even ridden in a race yet. But I will. And when I ride in races, I'm going to win—just like Ashleigh. You can bet on that, boy."

2

CINDY SAT WITH SAMANTHA IN THE BACKSEAT OF MIKE AND Ashleigh's big truck as they drove out to the training farm. She gazed out the window at the flat Miami countryside as it rolled past her window. But Cindy barely noticed the scenery. Instead she was replaying every second of her morning ride.

I passed the gate test, but did I really ride my absolute best? she wondered. *I'll need to in a race.*

"Earth to Cindy!" Samantha said.

With a jolt Cindy realized that someone was talking to her. "What?" she asked.

Samantha laughed. "You're so out of it! I was trying to tell you that I called Tor from the track—he says congratulations." Tor Nelson was Samantha's longtime boyfriend. He owned a jumping stable near Lexington. "What were you spacing out about?" she asked.

"Oh, I was just wondering how Champion is doing at the training farm." Cindy didn't want to make too much out of her gate test that morning. After all, for a real jockey, breaking a horse from the gate was all in a day's work. Cindy knew that everyone at Whitebrook simply expected her to become a great jockey. It was what she had been working toward for years.

But Ashleigh glanced back at Cindy and smiled. Cindy was sure Ashleigh knew what she had really been thinking about.

"Champion's doing great—but the rest of us are a little worn out keeping him happy," Mike told Cindy, turning the truck onto a dirt road.

"Any new Champion stories?" Cindy asked with a grin. She hadn't seen much of her beloved horse over the winter because she'd had to stay at home in Kentucky and go to school, but she kept close tabs on him.

"Only one—but it's a near-disaster story," Ashleigh said. "Yesterday a deliveryman brought in new bags of feed. Champion's tack trunk was in the way, so the deliveryman pushed it closer to Champion's stall. Champion opened the trunk—"

"He waited, of course, until no one was around," Mike added.

"Champion got into his brushes and other equipment," Ashleigh went on. "He shredded the brushes and ripped his finishing cloths to bits. I didn't yell at him because I was too worried. I was so afraid he'd eaten something and would get sick."

"He never eats anything he gets into," Cindy remarked. Champion was the most mischievous horse she knew but also the smartest.

"That's true," Ashleigh agreed. "But I couldn't help worrying for two days."

"In short, Champion's fine," Mike said with a laugh as he parked the truck in front of the spacious training facility.

"We're finally here!" Cindy quickly hopped out of the truck. She longed to see Champion after their two-month separation, and she also wanted to look around. She had never seen the training farm.

The farm was surrounded by thick orange groves, stretching off in all directions and broken only by riding trails. At the center were three long rows of tidy white barns for the horses in training. A mile-long dirt training track was situated to the right of the barns. The farm owner's modest, one-story stucco home was screened by palm trees.

Cindy didn't see much action on the track. Most of the horses seemed to be in their stalls for the afternoon. But in front of one barn Cindy spotted a colt grazing in the sunshine, quickly moving from patch

13

to patch of grass. He was pulling Len, Whitebrook's farm manager, along with him.

Cindy laughed. She would have recognized Champion from a mile away. With his finely arched neck and gleaming chocolate coat, the colt's beauty stood out against the bright blue Florida sky. But it was the coiled energy of all Champion's movements that instantly gave him away to Cindy.

"Champion!" she called. "I'm here, boy!"

The colt's head shot up. He stood frozen, legs braced, his wide-set dark eyes fixed on her. A breeze ruffled his flowing, almost black mane and tail.

Cindy ran toward him. "It's really me!" she said.

With a short whinny Champion bobbed his head— then began dragging Len in Cindy's direction.

"All right, I'm not going to argue with you," the older man said with a smile as the determined colt reached Cindy.

Cindy hugged her horse tight, pressing her cheek against his shining neck. "I'm so glad to see you," she whispered, overcome with emotion. Ashleigh had called home almost daily with reports on Champion, but second-hand news didn't compare with being together again.

Champion craned his neck to nudge her fondly. Cindy stepped back to look him over. The dark chestnut colt, with his imperious gaze and regal bearing, looked every inch the Triple Crown champion that he was. Cindy's heart swelled with pride.

"You look relaxed—for you, I mean," she said. Cindy knew that the atmosphere was less stressful at the training farm than at the track. Both the backside and the racetrack itself were much more crowded with horses and riders, and the pressure was on to win races.

"I think the horses like it here," Samantha said. "They have to work to prepare for their races, but at the same time it's like a winter spa for them."

"The farm even has a swimming pool for the horses, to condition them," Ashleigh added.

"Did you take Champion in?" Cindy asked. The colt was standing close beside her, lazily rubbing his ear on her arm. Cindy loved the trust her horse had in her. He might be the world's Triple Crown winner, but to her he was still Champion, the colt she had loved since the day he was born.

Ashleigh laughed. "No, I didn't take Champion swimming. I think he might enjoy it, but I don't trust him. The horses are supposed to swim in place, and it's hard to imagine Champion doing that. Remember what he did to the hot walker?"

Cindy grinned. "I don't think I'd put him on the hot walker again unless I wanted to break it." Usually Cindy cooled Champion out by walking him on a lead line. But one day she had been late for school and had tried to save time by clipping Champion to the hot walker. The hot walker was a mechanical

15

device that looked like a Ferris wheel lying on its side. The horses were clipped by their halters to spokes that pulled them around in a circle at a walk until they were cool.

Champion hadn't liked the hot walker. Either he didn't like being pulled around, or he had resented Cindy's sudden and unexpected departure. Champion had promptly dug in his heels and walked the wrong way while the hot walker's motor ground and strained in protest.

"I'm going to bring out Limitless," Ashleigh said. "Cindy, do you want to go for a trail ride with me before we move the horses? You could take Champion, and I'll ride Limitless. We've got time, and the horses might van better if they're exercised."

Cindy smiled broadly. She could hardly wait to get back in Champion's saddle—she hadn't ridden him in months. "Great, let's go," Cindy said, taking Champion's lead line from Len. Champion tossed his elegant head, then trotted eagerly after her, as if to say, Finally I'm going to see some action! Ashleigh followed, shaking her head and smiling.

Cindy crosstied the colt in the broad aisle of the spacious barn. The walls were made of stone, and the barn was cool and quiet. "I'll bet you enjoyed it here, boy," Cindy said as she slipped the bit into Champion's mouth. Champion had only left the training farm once that winter, to race in a seven-

16

furlong minor stakes at Gulfstream. He'd beaten the competition by eight lengths. His next race would be the Donn Handicap, a grade-one stakes at a mile and an eighth, also at Gulfstream.

"I think he's had a good time," Ashleigh said as she adjusted Limitless's saddle. "But now it's time to get to work."

After this ride we'll work, Cindy thought as she led Champion to the barn door. The bright yellow sunshine spilled over the colt's deep brown coat.

"Want a hand up, Cindy?" Mike offered.

"Sure, thanks," Cindy said. She quickly jumped into the saddle, using Mike's hand for leverage.

"Be careful, Cindy," Ashleigh said as she swung into the saddle. "Champion's been here at the training farm a couple of months, and I've taken him out on the trails, but parts of them will still be unfamiliar to him. And even though the training farm isn't as busy as the track, there's still plenty of action around here. Keep him away from other horses."

"I will." Cindy gripped her reins tightly. The moment she sat in the saddle she could feel the difference between riding Champion and Black Reason or one of the other more easygoing Whitebrook horses. Champion quivered with unreleased energy, and Cindy loved the comfortable feel of the saddle beneath her and the promise of the colt's power.

Ashleigh led the way to a broad trail cut through

the thick groves of orange trees. Champion lightly trotted after Ashleigh and Limitless and passed them. "You don't want to be second even on a trail ride, do you?" Cindy asked with a laugh.

"Hold him back," Ashleigh warned. "We're not out here to race."

Cindy gathered her reins to check Champion. The colt dropped his pace before she could apply pressure, as if he knew what she wanted. Champion skittered sideways a bit as he trotted slowly past the orange trees. But Cindy enjoyed the colt's high spirits. She knew that was one of the reasons he was the champion he was.

She leaned forward to run both hands along Champion's glossy neck. "I still haven't told you about the wonderful thing that happened today, Champion," she said. "I passed my gate test! I'm on my way to being a real jockey. What do you think about that?"

Champion cocked back one ear, listening to her voice.

"I think he's pleased," Ashleigh said with a smile.

"I'm just so glad to be with him again." Cindy sat deep in the saddle, melting into the experience of being back on her horse. *Every single stride of Champion's is so perfect*, she thought. *Black Reason's great to ride, but he just doesn't move like my Triple Crown Champion!*

Cindy smiled, daydreaming about riding Champion in a race someday, at Gulfstream or one of the other major tracks. She pictured herself in Arabia, at the Dubai World Cup, racing Champion across the burning, endless sands. A hot desert wind whipped through her hair under the glaring yellow ball of the sun. . . .

Champion snatched at an orange-tree branch, pulling her out of her daydream. Caught off balance, Cindy almost fell. She gripped Champion's mane and sat upright again. Luckily Ashleigh was riding a little ahead and didn't seem to have noticed.

"Can I pick an orange?" Cindy asked.

"I don't think anyone is going to miss it if you do," Ashleigh replied, looking back. "I see about twenty thousand of them all around us."

Before Cindy could reach for an orange, Champion stretched out his neck and grabbed an orange from the branch of the nearest tree for himself.

"Champion, what are you doing?" Cindy asked, laughing. "Are you really going to eat that orange? It's not even peeled."

She tipped sideways in the saddle to look around the colt's neck. Champion was holding the orange in his mouth, tossing his head a little. He bit into the orange.

"He does that all the time," Ashleigh said. "He learned to like orange juice in Florida."

"Figures." Cindy watched the colt relish his orange. She noticed that he was biting it carefully, squeezing out the juice but avoiding the rind. Champion certainly liked new experiences. He was such a character, Cindy thought. She loved his personality as much as his racing ability. "So how do you feel about Champion's chances in the Donn?" she asked Ashleigh. Cindy had read in the racing papers that Champion was expected to win, but she wanted to hear it from Ashleigh.

"It's going to be a challenging race, but nothing he can't handle, I think," Ashleigh said. "Dawn's Light will be there, and Saint Southern, but Champion's beaten both of them before. He hasn't had any more trouble with that hoof he injured in the Preakness."

"That's good." Cindy breathed a sigh of relief. She had hoped that the cut Champion had suffered to his right front hoof was just a minor injury, not a chronic problem. "So it's clear sailing for Champion," she said.

"For now." Ashleigh frowned. "The Donn is Champion's last race before the Dubai World Cup. It's not a bad prep in some ways—it's a mile and an eighth against good competition, and he should be in great form afterward. But the Nad al Sheba track in the United Arab Emirates is sand, and I don't know how to prepare him for that surface. Champion may not take to it."

Cindy nodded. "I guess we won't know until we try," she said.

"That's right," Ashleigh agreed. "We'll transport Champion to the track after the Donn, leaving enough time for him to get used to the desert climate and the sand."

"I hope he doesn't lose." Cindy knew that the eyes of the world would be on the race. Champion was the best horse in the country, but in Dubai he would face the top horses from Europe, Asia, and Arabia as well.

"Me too," Ashleigh replied. "It's going to be a challenge for him and for the jockey, too."

"I bet Champion can do it," Cindy said confidently. "And you're the best, Ashleigh. I'm going to work as hard as I can to try to ride like you."

Ashleigh smiled. "You've got talent, Cindy. You just need to learn how to use it. But you will."

Cindy glowed at Ashleigh's praise, glancing shyly at her. Cindy noticed that Limitless had increased his pace slightly so that the two colts were neck and neck again. She knew that Ashleigh must have given Limitless some kind of signal, but it was so subtle, Cindy hadn't even seen it. *Ashleigh's probably the best rider in the world,* Cindy thought.

"Do you still think it's a thrill to be a jockey?" she asked. "Or do you get used to it?"

"It's thrilling, all right." Ashleigh grinned. "When you're out on a racetrack with a crowded field of thousand-pound Thoroughbreds breathing down your neck from all sides, you're always plenty thrilled."

Cindy nodded and Ashleigh continued. "There's a lot of pressure on the track. It's not like galloping at Whitebrook with just one or two other horses. But I'll never really get over the wonder of racing," Ashleigh told her with a smile. "There's no feeling like it. And to ride a horse like Wonder or Champion is absolutely incredible. Both of them have so much speed and heart."

"I know." Cindy never forgot how lucky she was even to live at Whitebrook, with barns and paddocks full of gorgeous Thoroughbreds. Riding them was the icing on the cake.

"We should probably head back if Champion's had enough oranges," Ashleigh said. "I'd like to get the horses vanned over to the track and settled before dark."

"He doesn't seem to want any more." Champion had dropped his orange after squeezing out the juice. Now he was stealthily increasing the speed of his trot until he was almost cantering. Even Champion's fast trot was so smooth, Cindy didn't have any trouble sitting to it.

She decided to let him have his way. If Cindy had learned anything about Champion in four years, it was that she shouldn't fight him all the time, over every little thing. The colt needed to get his way once in a while.

Cindy noticed that Limitless was matching

Champion stride for stride. *He's a beautiful, talented horse,* she said to herself. She knew that any horse who won a stakes race was an exceptional horse, and Limitless had won two of them. It was just his bad luck that he was the same age as Champion and would always be compared to him. *He'd never be able to compete against Champion in a race unless a great jockey like Ashleigh rode him!* Cindy thought. *And Ashleigh can't ride both Champion and him at the same time.*

"Ian's already got the trailer pulled around," Ashleigh said. "We can just load Limitless and Champion—they're not hot."

"I hope they feel as good as I do." Cindy rotated her shoulders, loosening her grip on Champion's smooth, well-oiled leather reins. Cindy felt the deep contentment that she always felt at the end of a ride with Champion. She understood the difficult, high-strung colt and always seemed to know what he was thinking. When they went for rides together, they moved as one.

She untacked Champion next to the trailer and led him to the left stall. "Up, boy," she said, motioning to the ramp.

Champion marched right into the trailer. Mike had stocked the colt's feed tray with apples, carrots, and hay at Cindy's suggestion. She knew the horses expected those treats.

Ashleigh quickly loaded Limitless next to Champion. "Here we go!" she said. "It's back to the big time for them."

"I wish it was for me, too," Cindy murmured. She sighed, wishing that she could ride Champion on the track instead of just the training farm. *Once we get back to Gulfstream, I'll just be Champion's groom again*, she realized. She opened the trailer window to check on the colt. Champion promptly stuck out his elegant head. He had already finished his snacks and seemed to be asking for more.

"I wish I could ride you in the Dubai World Cup," Cindy murmured as she ran to a nearby orange tree to pick Champion just one more treat. "I could once I get my license. What a great birthday present that would be." Cindy had noticed a long time ago that this year the Dubai World Cup was on March 25, just four days before her sixteenth birthday.

Champion whinnied, fixing his bright eyes on the orange. Cindy laughed and shook her head to clear away her daydreams. "Right—I've never even ridden in a race, and I want to ride in the biggest race in the world. Of course Ashleigh will ride you, Champion. At least I'll get to go to Dubai as your groom."

But as Cindy fed the eager colt his orange, she couldn't help feeling that deep down she wanted more—that she desperately wanted to ride Champion in Dubai.

3

"WE'RE HOME!" LATE SUNDAY NIGHT CINDY DROPPED HER bag in the hall of her family's cottage at Whitebrook and stretched out her arms luxuriously.

"I thought we'd never make it," Samantha said wearily, setting her bag beside Cindy's. "What an awful flight!"

Their plane out of Miami had been delayed due to a mechanical problem. Cindy, Ashleigh, Samantha, Beth, Kevin, and Len had sat for hours in the cold, sterile airport waiting room. Luckily Kevin had gone to sleep and missed most of the ordeal. Christina was still at the track with Mike and Ian.

Beth yawned and shifted Kevin to her other arm.

25

"I'm going to put Kevin to bed—and me. It's after one in the morning."

"I'm going, too." Samantha followed Beth to the stairs. Cindy looked at her mother and sister as they started to walk up the stairs. She could barely see Kevin's small face peeking out of the blanket Beth had wrapped him in.

"I'll be up in a few minutes," she told them. "I want to see the horses for a little while."

Beth stopped walking and frowned for a moment, but Samantha nodded. "Just lock the door when you come back in," she said.

"Don't stay too long, Cindy," Beth said, sounding resigned. "You're already going to be a zombie at school tomorrow."

"I know." Cindy wanted to get *some* sleep because in only three hours she'd be exercise-riding Honor Bright. The spirited filly needed careful riding. The beautiful two-year-old daughter of Townsend Princess and granddaughter of Wonder was headed for races this summer.

I'll just take one look at Honor, Glory, and Glory's Joy, Cindy thought, opening the cottage door and stepping outside. Glory's Joy was Glory's very first foal. Now a yearling, the pretty gray filly looked much like her sire. She was one of Cindy's favorites.

Cindy gasped as the frigid winter air burned her lungs. A half-moon spilled blue-white light on the grass and dirt, which was glittering with frost.

She walked quickly, her boots slipping a little on patches of snow. *I'd better get to the barn before I change my mind about being out!* she thought. *I can't believe how cold it is here. But I should get used to it—it's not going to be much warmer in a couple of hours when I ride.*

The training barn glowed in a halo of orange from the streetlight. Cindy stepped into the warm barn and peered through the semidarkness. The horses were mostly quiet and sleeping. She could hear soft sighs and the crackle of straw as a horse shifted position.

"Honor?" Cindy called softly as she approached the filly's stall.

A moment later Honor thrust her exquisite head over the half door. The bay filly's almost perfect star gleamed in the dim light.

"That's a girl," Cindy whispered as she approached the stall door. "I'm back, sweetheart."

Honor Bright snorted and backed away from the stall door. Cindy narrowed her eyes and blew out a breath, taking in the filly's exquisite good looks. Like Wonder and Princess, Honor was just over fifteen hands, small for a Thoroughbred, but she was perfectly proportioned. Her head, with its broad forehead and tapering muzzle, was one of the prettiest Cindy had ever seen.

Honor dropped her black muzzle to sniff Cindy's hands. "Yes, it's me," Cindy said. "Guess what—

we're going for a ride tomorrow. It'll be your first ride since we took you out of training for the winter. You'll like that, won't you?"

Honor leaned affectionately into her caresses, as if to say she'd like to do anything with Cindy.

Cindy sighed as she looked the lovely filly over one last time. "I wish I could ride you in your races, too, instead of only being your exercise-rider." She frowned. "Wasn't I just saying that about Champion? I want to ride you in your races so much," she said softly. "But I'm sure Ashleigh will, and that has to be okay with me. Ashleigh has so much more experience, and she loves you, too."

Honor tentatively dropped her head on Cindy's shoulder, as if she sympathized.

Stop thinking like that, Cindy ordered herself. *You're incredibly lucky to have the chances you do. Honor will be racing for a long time—you may get to ride her someday.*

The barn was quiet, and Honor lowered her head, as if she might be falling asleep. Cindy yawned and rubbed her eyes.

"I won't visit Glory tonight," she said to herself. "I'd wake up the other stallions, and they'd make a lot of noise. And I bet Joy's asleep."

Cindy tore herself away from Honor and walked quickly back up to the cottage. *I stayed out here too late,* she thought remorsefully. The horizon glowed in the dark sky where the moon had set. Cindy stopped, her attention caught by a brilliant star blazing overhead.

"Star light, star bright, first star I see tonight . . ." Cindy smiled, feeling silly for thinking that she could get what she wanted simply by wishing upon a star. She knew that she usually accomplished her goals through hard work.

"But wishes can come true," she said aloud. "I got to exercise-ride Glory back when I hardly knew anything about Thoroughbreds. The only problem is, I wish for so much, I don't know where to begin."

Cindy looked back at the star. "I wish that I'll get to ride Champion in a race," she whispered. "And maybe even Honor, too."

A cold breeze sprang up, and the star twinkled even more fiercely in the black sky as if to answer her. Cindy shivered as the late night cold cut right through her jean jacket.

Did I get my wish? she wondered, hurrying toward the comforting yellow light of the cottage. *And if I did, which one?*

Just hours later, in the dim light of dawn, Cindy tried to stop her teeth from chattering while she led Honor out of her stall to brush her. Cindy had warmed up after doing her early morning chores—mucking out five stalls in the training barn and brushing three of the horses that would be exercised that day. But the damp cold of the cloudy day was already sinking into her bones again. As she put Honor in crossties Cindy's arms and back ached from all the shoveling.

"What's the matter, Cindy? Are you chilly?" teased Mark Collier, a groom and exercise-rider.

"I sure am." Cindy stamped her feet, trying to get the tingle out of her toes.

"It's hard to feel sorry for somebody who's cold in Kentucky because she's been hanging out in the Florida sunshine," Mark said with a grin.

"I know, I know." Cindy dug for a dandy brush in Honor's tack trunk. "I'll warm up again when I get Honor out on the track."

The sleek bay filly rolled her eye back at Cindy to watch her every move. "It's okay, girl," Cindy murmured as she ran the brush soothingly over Honor's shining back. Slowly the filly's tense muscles relaxed.

Len walked over to them from the stable office. "She's been a little off her feed," he said. "I don't know why."

"Maybe she missed you, Cindy," Mark joked.

Len nodded. "She's a sensitive filly. That could be."

Samantha led one of the three-year-olds, Golden Beam, toward the barn door. "Aren't you exhausted, Cindy?" she asked. "You didn't get much sleep last night. I know that you got up much earlier than me."

Cindy shook her head and reached for the tiny

exercise saddle Len held. There was no way she could let herself be sleepy now. She couldn't wait to take Honor for her first ride of the new year. She loved the filly, and riding Honor would be good practice. Sweet but spirited, Honor had already shown talent on the track last fall.

I'll be dying for sleep by about third period at school, but I'm not going to worry about that now, Cindy thought as she eased the bit into Honor's mouth. The filly tossed her head a little, but Cindy was able to slip the headpiece over Honor's ears. "Okay, girl, let's go," Cindy said.

Outside the barn she sprang lightly into the saddle from a mounting block. As they walked to the track Honor whuffed out quick breaths into the frigid air. Cindy squinted as the sun burst between the cloud banks, highlighting the filly's tawny brown coat with gold. She turned in the saddle to look for Ashleigh. Ashleigh would be supervising Honor and the other horses' exercise since Ian and Mike were still at the Gulfstream track with Champion.

"I hope Ashleigh thinks I do okay with you," Cindy murmured. "Ashleigh knows you're not easy to ride, and if you put in a good exercise session, she'll be impressed."

Honor's perfectly shaped ears pricked, and Cindy saw Ashleigh come out of the stallion barn and walk over to them.

"Let's give Honor a very easy session today," Ashleigh said, running a hand lightly over the filly's neck. "Walk and trot only. Watch her carefully, Cindy—you know how excitable she is."

"I will." Cindy pulled the strap of her helmet tight and pointed the bay filly at the gap of the track. She put Honor through her paces of a walk and trot, keeping her to the outside rail, where the horses moved more slowly.

Honor trotted confidently along, her neck bowed a little against Cindy's restraint. *She's going great*, Cindy thought as they swept into the backside. She looked over at the gap to see if Ashleigh had noticed.

Mark posted by on Beautiful Music, another two-year-old. Honor flung up her head and charged after the other filly.

Cindy snapped back to attention. "No, girl! Don't go faster than a trot!" Instantly she tightened up on the reins.

But the headstrong filly was galloping almost in place. Honor repeatedly tossed her head as she fought Cindy's restraint.

"Steady now." Cindy gripped the saddle tightly with her legs. She knew she could be in for a wild ride. *Please don't rear or bolt, Honor!* she pleaded silently. Cindy's breath came in quick gasps from the effort of holding back the powerful filly.

Finally Honor dropped back down into an unsteady, high-stepping trot. A heavy sweat darkened her neck.

"Sorry, Cindy!" Mark called from up the track.

"That's okay!" Cindy knew that it was her fault the filly had almost run off with her.

Cindy drew a deep breath as they approached the gap. Ashleigh had stepped out on the track to stop them. "Ashleigh's going to yell at me, Honor," she murmured. "I guess I deserve it."

But Ashleigh was smiling. "Honor's full of it today, isn't she?" Ashleigh asked. "But you did a good job out there, Cindy. You didn't let her get away from you."

Ashleigh didn't see why Honor tried to run away with me, Cindy realized with relief. *She doesn't know that I just wasn't paying attention.* Cindy straightened her shoulders. *I guess I did put in a pretty good ride once I realized we were in trouble,* she decided.

"Take Honor back to the barn and cool her out," Ashleigh said. "Then you have to go off to school, unfortunately. I've got a couple of other horses I could use help with."

"I'll get up earlier tomorrow so I have more time," Cindy said eagerly.

Ashleigh smiled at Cindy. "Well, okay. But don't kill yourself."

Cindy led Honor toward the barn. The filly followed willingly with her head down.

"You're so sweated up, and it's freezing." Cindy felt a stab of guilt a she rubbed Honor's wet shoulder. "I'll do better the next time, girl," she murmured. "I promise. I'll do whatever it takes to be a perfect rider, like Ashleigh."

Later that morning Cindy hurried through the empty halls at Henry Clay High School to her first-period English class. The bus had already left by the time she had Honor cooled out. Samantha had given Cindy a ride to school, but she was still late.

Mrs. Lattner, Cindy's English teacher, turned from the board to stare at Cindy. All twenty kids in the class swiveled to look at her, too. Max Smith, one of Cindy's best friends and the son of Whitebrook's vet, smiled sympathetically.

"Ms. McLean, so good of you to join us this morning," Mrs. Lattner said. "But I guess we should be happy you're here at all."

Blushing, Cindy slid into her seat next to Max. She had once tried to explain to Mrs. Lattner that sometimes her work with the horses made her late to school. The teacher had frowned and told Cindy that her studies were as important as the horses. Then she'd given Cindy detention for a week.

Cindy sighed. *I wonder if Mrs. Lattner will give me detention again*, she thought dejectedly.

"Where were you?" Max whispered as soon as Mrs. Lattner had turned back to the board.

Cindy watched the teacher carefully until she was sure Mrs. Lattner was busy diagramming the structure of a poem. "Working with the horses," she whispered back.

Mrs. Lattner turned quickly and looked out over the class. Cindy bent studiously over her poetry book, sitting on her hands to warm them. The weather outside was still cold, and the classroom seemed dark and drafty. *I miss Florida more than ever*, she thought, letting out a yawn. *I wish I could start riding in races right away like Ashleigh, instead of going to school.*

"Hey," Max whispered. Cindy looked over—Max was passing her a note under his desk. Mrs. Lattner was looking at the ceiling, lost in thought. Cindy grabbed the note.

I called you last night, Max had written. *I missed you. How was Florida?*

Cindy felt her face redden slightly as she read Max's note. Recently, Max had become more than a friend. Max and Cindy had sort of been seeing each other, although they had never officially discussed their relationship. Cindy suddenly realized that she hadn't really spoken to Max in a while. *But he knows that I've been busy*, she thought. *At least there's one reason it's good to be here instead of Miami—I get to see Max.*

She slid a book onto her lap to write on. *I know*, she

wrote, *I'm sorry I didn't call you back. We got in late last night, and I was busy with the horses.*

Cindy handed the note back to Max and then slouched in her seat as Mrs. Lattner droned on and on. *How am I going to get through six more periods?* Cindy thought. *School is such a drag.*

When English was finally over, she pushed through the desks to the door.

"Hey, Cindy, wait up," Max called.

Cindy stopped outside the classroom door and turned to face him. She thought about how cute he was as she looked into his bright green eyes. "How's it going?" she asked him.

Max shrugged. "Not bad. I guess not as exciting as your life has been. Not everyone gets to miss school to go to Florida," he teased.

Cindy laughed. "Yeah, I know. It really was hard work, though. But I guess since I got my jockey's license—"

"You passed!" Max interrupted her, giving her a big hug. "I knew you would—even though you were nervous about it. I can't believe that you didn't tell me right away."

Cindy pulled away from him. "I guess I'm just so sleepy that I forgot you didn't know yet," she said, stifling another yawn. "But isn't it great? My first race should be soon!"

"I'm really happy for you," Max told her. "And now that you're back, we can hang out."

"I'd like to ... but I *am* going to be really busy," Cindy answered.

Max's smile faded. "Are you saying that you don't have time for me?" he asked, sounding disappointed.

"No, it's not that. It's just ..." Cindy suddenly felt guilty—she didn't mean to hurt Max's feelings. But she also knew that if she wanted to become a top jockey, she had to devote most of her time to riding. *Max will eventually understand*, she told herself. "It's just, you know how important racing is to me," she explained to him. "It's going to take up a lot of my time. I want to hang out with you—I just don't know when I'll be able to."

Max opened his mouth to respond, but before he could say anything, Cindy's friends Heather Gilbert, Melissa Souter, and Laura Billings came up to them.

"Hey, there's the jockey!" Heather said, grinning. Heather shared Cindy's love of horses—she took jumping lessons at Tor's stable. Cindy often went over to the stable with Samantha to watch Heather's lessons. "Tor told me the good news," Heather explained, giving Cindy a warm hug.

"I can't believe that you're a jockey now!" Melissa said excitedly.

"I'm not a jockey yet," Cindy reminded them. "I still have to ride in a race, you know. And I've got a lot of work left to do before my first race," she added.

"Cindy, I'm glad that you got your license, but

could we please talk about something other than horses for a minute?" Laura asked, brushing her chestnut hair behind her shoulders. "We haven't set a date for our class skating party yet." Pretty, vivacious Laura was president of the tenth-grade social committee. Cindy and many of her friends were also on the committee.

"I thought Saturday, February 19, would be good," Heather said. "That's in three weeks, so we'd have time to plan."

"Well, let's do it," Melissa said eagerly. Melissa's parents owned a large training and breeding farm a few miles from Whitebrook. Melissa exercise-rode for her father.

"We'll plan it then. We haven't done any class activities for a while," Laura said, smiling.

"It'll be a lot of fun," Heather agreed. "What do you think, Cindy?"

Cindy's friends looked to her for a response. Cindy realized that she wasn't as enthusiastic about the skating party as everyone else was—she had too much on her mind.

"I think I'll probably be busy in late February," Cindy said absently. By then she would have ridden in her first race. If that went well, she would be busy preparing for her second race with Black Reason, or maybe even to ride Champion. Cindy couldn't picture that she would have time for a skating party.

Max rolled his eyes. "It'll just be for one afternoon, Cindy," he said. "You should be able to take that much time off."

"I don't really know yet." Cindy shrugged and leaned against the row of lockers behind her. "I'll just have to see how my riding goes."

Max stared at her. "Can't you make any plans?"

"Of course," Cindy began. "I already planned to get up an hour earlier tomorrow. That way I'll have more time to—"

The bell rang for second-period class. "Never mind," Max said over his shoulder as he walked down the hall to class. "I'll talk to you later—if you're not too busy."

"Max . . ." Cindy called after him, but he was already at the other end of the hall.

"Come on, let's go to gym," Heather said.

Max seemed annoyed, Cindy thought as she followed her friends and dragged her aching body to gym class. *But he'll come around. Besides, I have plenty of time to talk to him at school—it's not like I can ride here.*

"Cindy, do you have a minute?" Ashleigh called to Cindy that evening.

Cindy turned quickly, a bucket of feed in each hand. She had been just about to feed Honor and Calamity Jane, a gray two-year-old that Vic Teleski, one of Whitebrook's full-time exercise-riders, was bringing along as a racehorse. "Sure," she responded.

Ashleigh was looking out the doorway of the stable office with a serious expression on her face.

I wonder what Ashleigh wants. Cindy set down her buckets and walked back to the office.

"Come on in." Ashleigh gestured to a chair across from her desk in the office.

Cindy sat on the edge of the chair and clenched her hands. Ashleigh was searching for something in the piles of paper on her desk.

Ashleigh looked up with a smile and handed Cindy the conditions book for Gulfstream Park, listing all the races the track would be running for the winter-spring meet. She had circled a race in red.

"Six-furlong allowance race, three-year-olds and upward, twenty thousand dollars," Cindy read. She looked up at Ashleigh. "It's on Donn Handicap day. Which of our horses is running in it?" Cindy could feel her heart begin to beat faster.

"Would you like to ride Black Reason in that race?" Ashleigh asked. "I'll be there, of course, riding Champion in the Donn."

"Wow!" Cindy sputtered. "Of course!" She had known Ashleigh would come up with a race for her, but on Donn Handicap day! The crowds would be huge, and only the very best horses would run.

"Do you think you'll be ready to ride so soon?"

Ashleigh asked. "Donn day is in less than two weeks. I discussed it with Ian and Beth, and you wouldn't be able to leave school until a week from next Tuesday. That only gives you Wednesday through Friday to work with Black Reason. It's not a lot of time, I know."

"No problem!" Cindy said eagerly. "I'll do whatever it takes. And I've worked with Black Reason so much before, here at Whitebrook—I'll be ready." Cindy couldn't stop smiling.

Ashleigh nodded and rose from her chair. "Good," she said. "We'll work out the details later."

Cindy stepped outside the office and squeezed her eyes tightly shut, wanting to hold on to the happiness of this moment forever. *It's really going to happen*, she thought. *I'm going to ride in a race! I can hardly believe it!*

Honor whinnied softly from down the aisle. A moment later Calamity Jane echoed her call.

Cindy's eyes snapped open. She realized she had totally forgotten the two hungry young horses. "I'm coming, girls," she called.

Cindy poured Calamity's grain into her box, then stepped to the stall next door to fill Honor's. The bay filly dug deep into her dinner.

"Honor, did you hear my good news?" Cindy asked happily. Honor glanced up, then returned to munching her feed. "Ashleigh and I are riding in races on the same day." Cindy leaned on her elbows over Honor's half door, a broad smile stealing over her face. "Do you know how great it will be when we both win for Whitebrook?"

4

CINDY WOKE UP VERY EARLY THE NEXT MORNING TO NEAR total blackness. She could barely see the silhouette of the trees outside her window, illuminated by the faint glow of the streetlight. Rolling over, Cindy saw that her alarm clock read three A.M.

"Good, I didn't oversleep," she whispered, throwing back the covers. She quickly put on a pair of jeans and layered on a T-shirt, sweatshirt, and riding vest. After lacing up a pair of low jodhpur boots, she tiptoed down the stairs.

In the deserted kitchen Cindy broke a banana off the bunch and opened the outside door. The sky was pitch-black everywhere, without the faintest glow promising sunrise on the horizon. Clouds hid the stars, and the air was heavy and moist.

Cindy set out determinedly for the training barn. Her boots crunched solidly on the gravel path, seeming to make the only sound in the world. She shivered as the damp cold crept under her clothes. "It's weird to be up this early," she said to herself. "But I have so much to do today."

Cindy had lain awake the previous night, thinking about her upcoming race. She wanted to do everything she could to prepare for it. She had decided the best thing to do would be to ride as many horses as possible every day. That would not only get her in top shape, but would also ready her to take on all the different horses in her race.

The barn, usually so bustling, was utterly still. Cindy walked down the dimly lit aisle, passing sleeping horses. "Wow, I'm here before Ashleigh," she murmured. "That's a first." *Ashleigh is so dedicated to her work,* Cindy thought. *But it's my work now, too.* She vowed to be more disciplined.

Cindy could hear Honor restlessly moving in her stall at the end of the barn. "I'll brush you first, but I think I want to ride you last," she said. "I'll warm up on the other horses and give you my very best." Cindy frowned. Was that how she should do this? *I guess so, if I'm not too exhausted after all those other rides,* she decided. *I'll have to pace myself.*

Cindy began her morning chores with determination, rapidly mucking out stalls. The aches in her arms and back from the day before disappeared as she worked. She was surprised at how quickly she finished. "I guess I can go faster when I just put my mind to it," she said aloud.

"Good morning, Cindy." Ashleigh was walking down the stable aisle. She seemed a little surprised to see Cindy there already.

"Morning." Cindy replaced the wheelbarrow, shovel, and rake in the tack room and walked to the office. She needed to check out her plans with Ashleigh. Cindy knew they were a little unusual.

Ashleigh had left the office and was standing in front of Fleet Street's stall, petting the filly. The black two-year-old daughter of Fleet Goddess was about the same age as Honor. "What's up, Cindy?" Ashleigh asked.

"I was just wondering what your plans are for me today," Cindy said.

Ashleigh smiled. "Well, if you're here this early, *you* must have plans. What did you have in mind?"

"I'm almost done with my chores, and so I thought I could get started riding," Cindy began.

Ashleigh raised an eyebrow. "You really must have gotten up early! When did you get to the barn—around four?"

"Earlier than that. But you get here almost that

early every day," Cindy told her. She wondered why Ashleigh seemed to expect less of her than she did of herself. "I don't want to slack off now that I'm trying to become a real jockey," Cindy added. "I've got a lot to do."

"But Cindy, this is my full-time job," Ashleigh pointed out. "I don't have school and after-school activities like you do."

I wish I didn't have those, either! Cindy thought. "I've put the after-school activities on hold for now," she explained. "That way I can spend more time on the job."

"I'm not sure that's wise," Ashleigh said, furrowing her brow. "I don't want to lecture you, but at your age spending time with friends and doing well in school is important. I'm married and have a family. This is my life."

"But it's mine, too!" Cindy burst out.

"Not quite in the same way." Ashleigh was silent for a moment. "You haven't been spending time with Max lately. What does he think about all this?" she asked.

"He understands," Cindy said. She paused for a moment. "I mean, I think he understands . . . or he will eventually."

Ashleigh looked at her for a few seconds. "Well, it's fine to be driven. Just be careful not to lose perspective."

"I know," Cindy told her, shifting impatiently from foot to foot. Ashleigh was spending a lot of precious time talking. Cindy was all too aware that she had to leave the horses and deal with school and the rest of her life in just a few short hours.

"What was on your agenda for today?" Ashleigh asked.

"I thought that I'd ride not just Honor but Fleet Street and Lucky Chance, too." Lucky Chance was the two-year-old daughter of Shining. "If that's okay with you," Cindy added quickly.

Ashleigh looked at her quizzically. "That's a lot of riding on a school day."

"But I've got time since I'm here so early," Cindy pleaded. Usually Ashleigh gave great advice. But she just didn't seem to understand how badly Cindy wanted to win her first race. *Ashleigh's been a jockey so long, she just takes it for granted*, Cindy thought. *She's forgotten how I feel.*

Ashleigh sighed. "Well, I suppose I could use some help with Fleet Street. Lucky Chance is going well for Samantha, so I don't really want to switch riders."

"I don't have to ride either of them if you really don't want me to," Cindy said. She suddenly realized that she was a little out of line, trying to give Ashleigh training directions.

"It's not that. You just caught me off guard." Ashleigh nodded briskly. "No, I think it would be fine if you rode Fleet Street. Just keep an eye on her, Cindy. She's as young as Honor, and you don't know her as well."

"I'll be careful. Thanks, Ashleigh!" Cindy stepped over to the filly's stall and clipped a lead line to her halter. She had already groomed Fleet Street and set out her tack by the stall door.

Fleet Street followed her willingly to the crossties. Fleet Street had her mother's finely molded head and small star, but the compact black filly had none of her dam's legginess. Cindy had never ridden her, but she seemed to be a quiet, well-mannered young horse.

"Ashleigh wasn't too happy with my plan," Cindy said to Fleet Street as she adjusted the exercise saddle on the filly's back. "But, maybe if I do this every day, she'll get used to it."

Fleet Street lightly pawed the aisle, as if to say she was raring to go, too.

"Well, if it isn't Miss Rise and Shine!" teased Mark as he brought Freedom's Ring out of his stall. Cindy knew that Mark was riding the black four-year-old colt, usually one of Vic's, while Vic was at Gulfstream.

"Oh, did you just get here?" Cindy joked back. "The horses and I have been up for hours!"

"Yeah, yeah." Mark crosstied Freedom, facing Fleet Street. "When did you really get here?"

"Quarter after three." Cindy tightened the girth on Fleet Street's saddle. "I wanted to get my chores done early."

"You've got to be kidding." Mark stared at Cindy in disbelief. "When do you sleep?"

"In school," Cindy said flippantly.

"I'll bet you do. How long are you going to keep this up?"

"Till I win my first race," Cindy said patiently. "Maybe longer." She couldn't believe that everyone was so shocked that she was working hard.

"You're crazy; do you know that?" Mark asked.

Cindy smiled to herself. In just a few short weeks he'd see how well her plan had worked—when she was standing with Black Reason in the winner's circle.

"What are you doing with Fleet Street?" Mark asked as Cindy bridled the filly.

"What does it look like? I'm going to ride her!" Cindy knew that Mark wouldn't mind her teasing tone. He was only twenty—not that much older than she was—and they were friends.

"I've ridden Fleet Street a couple of times. She's a nice filly," Mark commented.

Cindy glanced down the aisle. Honor was hanging her head over the stall door and scratching her chin against the wood. She seemed to be wondering why Cindy was taking out another horse. "Don't worry,

Honor—we'll go out in a little while," Cindy called. "I promise."

Fleet Street followed Cindy quietly down the barn aisle. She was used to attention from Cindy and other people. The filly seemed easily to accept the change in rider.

In the office Cindy saw on the board that Fleet Street was scheduled only to walk and trot, not to gallop. *That's not much of a workout for me!* she thought, disappointed.

Fleet Street nuzzled her affectionately, as if to say she would enjoy whatever Cindy had planned. Cindy patted her star. "You're right. Let's do our best no matter what it is."

Cindy led Fleet Street to a mounting block outside the barn. She was almost surprised to see that the sun had finally risen. The day was cloudy and cool, and the ground was damp. "That's just dew," Cindy said to herself. "I doubt if the track's slippery." She swung into the saddle. "We should do all right, girl."

At the track Mark was already circling Freedom at a trot. The black colt had won an allowance race at Belmont and a grade-three stakes at Saratoga last summer, but then he had lost his next two races. Ian and Mike had decided to give him the winter off and try him again that spring.

Cindy aimed Fleet Street toward the outside rail. The filly moved off obediently, stepping close to the rail. Cindy let out the reins a little and relaxed in the saddle.

"How are you doing?" Mark called from behind her.

"Okay. I'm a little tired after all those chores," Cindy replied. "This is going to be a long day."

"Well, keep Fleet Street in hand," Mark said. "I'm going to gallop Freedom."

"I will." Fleet Street walked briskly, keeping the perfect distance from the rail. Cindy saw Ashleigh climb up on the fence near the gap to watch them.

The bobbing motion of the filly's energetic walk was soothing. Cindy let up on the reins a little to rest her arms. The aches had returned full force. She closed her eyes briefly, willing the grainy, tired feeling in them to go away.

The next second Cindy almost fell out of the saddle backward as Fleet Street took off at a roaring gallop. "No, girl!" Cindy cried, but it was too late. Instinctively Cindy tightened her reins and tried to regain her balance. She saw Freedom passing them at a slow gallop on the inside. *Mark told me he was going to gallop!* she thought in dismay. *I should have been ready for Fleet Street to take off after him. Where was my head?*

Fleet Street pulled hard on the reins and continued to gallop jerkily, showing herself to be the racehorse that she was. Cindy quickly sat up straight in the saddle. "Whoa, girl," she called. "Nice and slow."

The filly finally responded, slowing to a trot, then relaxing into a sprightly, even walk. Cindy quickly bent to adjust her stirrup. Her foot had pushed through it during the filly's erratic gallop.

"That wasn't a good ride at all," Cindy muttered. She hardly dared to look over at Ashleigh.

Cindy moved the filly up into a trot, this time focusing on her every movement. "I hope Ashleigh doesn't think I was careless with you just because you're not mine," Cindy said ruefully. "I'm sorry, girl." Fleet Street trotted steadily along, as if to say that she had her mind on business now, too.

After they had circled the track, Cindy pulled up the filly at the gap. Cindy forced herself to meet Ashleigh's eyes. "I'm really sorry," Cindy said. "I guess she caught me napping out there."

"She did." Ashleigh stroked Fleet Street's black velvet neck. The filly dropped her head to lip Ashleigh's hand. "You had me worried for a second," Ashleigh told her.

Cindy felt terrible. She knew only too well how close she and Fleet Street had come to total disaster. A runaway horse on the track could easily injure itself or another horse. "I'll watch out with Honor," she promised.

"I would," Ashleigh agreed. "I don't know if you'd get a second chance with her."

Feeling Ashleigh's rebuke, Cindy led Fleet Street

toward the barn. *What if something had happened to Ashleigh's favorite filly?* Cindy thought. *I'd never forgive myself. I have to do better than that!*

"Cindy!" Mark walked up behind her with Freedom. "I'll take care of Fleet Street if you want to get going with Honor," he said.

"Oh, I'd better take care of her." Cindy kicked the dirt with the toe of her boot. "It's the least I can do after the way I screwed up out there."

"Don't take it so hard," Mark said gently. "Everybody makes mistakes. Freedom and I didn't mean to crowd you."

"I know. You didn't—you told me you were going to gallop. I have to get used to riding in traffic for races, anyway."

Mark reached for Fleet Street's reins. Cindy hesitated. She knew Fleet Street deserved extra attention. But if Cindy dawdled here, she wouldn't have time to ride Honor before school. She nodded. "Thanks, Mark," she said. "I owe you one."

"No problem," he assured her.

Cindy ran quickly back to the barn to get Honor for her exercise. Samantha was brushing Lucky Chance in crossties. "Hi, Cindy," she said. "Are you going to take out Honor?"

"Yeah, right now." Honor was pacing around her stall, stopping every few seconds to pop her head over the door to look for Cindy. *I can't wait to get out on the track with her,* Cindy thought. Spirited, graceful Honor was definitely her own favorite filly.

Cindy clipped a lead rope to Honor's halter and groaned. The filly was covered with bits of straw. "Honor, why did you have to roll? Don't you know we're in a hurry?"

Honor tossed her beautiful head, looking pleased with herself.

Cindy hurriedly crosstied the filly and ran a dandy brush over her, then tacked her up. Cindy knew the grooming job wasn't perfect, but she was out of time if she still wanted to get in a ride. *I'll do everything right tomorrow,* Cindy promised herself.

She lightly hopped into the saddle and picked up her stirrups with her boots. Honor was scheduled for a gallop. Smiling broadly, Cindy rubbed the filly's neck and asked her to walk toward the track. Honor set a brisk pace, her black hooves sinking into the soft ground.

"Ready, Cindy?" Ashleigh asked as Cindy rode through the gap.

"You bet," Cindy said confidently.

She put Honor through her warm-up walk and trot. Even at the slow gaits a sheen of sweat broke out on the excited filly's neck. "Steady, girl," Cindy said softly. "Save it. We'll gallop in just another furlong."

As if she understood, Honor dropped her pace. The exquisite filly seemed to float through the misty gray day. Cindy smiled with bliss as she moved with the supple young horse. *Nothing beats this*, she thought. She forgot her aches and pains, the bad ride on Fleet Street, and her worries about how well she would do in a race. She and her horse were alone on the chilly morning, a bright streak moving through a world of gray and damp.

She looked ahead. No horses were in their path. On the far side of the track Samantha was circling Lucky Chance. "Okay, girl," Cindy said. "Ready for a gallop?"

Seeming to understand Cindy's words, Honor swept instantly into a gallop, her hoofbeats quick and staccato as she dug into the ground. Honor swung around the far turn, gaining speed.

"Way to go, Cindy!" Samantha called from the outside rail.

Honor started at Samantha's voice. She threw up her head and dropped off the pace.

"No, you don't," Cindy murmured. She leaned forward in the saddle, urging Honor on with her seat, her hands buried in the filly's glossy neck for balance and to ask for speed.

Honor's gallop smoothed out again, and Cindy smiled triumphantly. She let the filly gallop out another furlong, then pulled her back down to a walk as they passed the gap.

"Very good, Cindy." The concern in Ashleigh's

face had disappeared, and she was nodding approvingly.

"That was a great exercise session, Honor," Cindy said, leaning forward to press her cheek against Honor's sleek golden brown neck. "If I can keep it up, I'll be set for my race, and everybody will think so. But just to make sure, I'll get up even earlier tomorrow."

5

"CINDY!" MRS. LATTNER'S LOUD VOICE SUDDENLY WOKE Cindy up the next morning in English class.

Cindy jerked up her head. She had been resting her head in her hands for just a moment, looking down at her English book on the desk. *I fell asleep!* she thought. *Now what do I do? I don't even know what Mrs. Lattner asked me!*

The teacher folded her arms and tapped her foot impatiently. "Do you have an answer?"

Cindy didn't think Mrs. Lattner would appreciate it if she asked her to repeat the question. Cindy had been in her own world, dreaming about her morning workout. That morning she had gotten up at a quarter of three. Still, Cindy felt that she never got enough done to prepare for her race.

Today Ashleigh had let Cindy take out Fleet Street and Honor again. Cindy felt satisfied that she had ridden well, but she was so tired, she didn't have much fun. For the first time in her life she was glad to get off a horse when she finished up with Honor.

Each day getting out of bed was harder. To get even seven hours of sleep, Cindy had to be in bed at night by eight o'clock. That was impossible with schoolwork.

And now Mrs. Lattner is pressuring me even more, Cindy thought as she looked at the teacher's stern face. *She'll never understand what I'm trying to do!*

"Talk to me after class," Mrs. Lattner said, turning back to the blackboard.

Cindy groaned silently. *Here comes detention!*

Max leaned over. "I couldn't wake you up," he whispered. "You were really out."

Cindy didn't say anything back; she just nodded. All she needed was to be caught talking.

Max shrugged and sat back. For the rest of the class Cindy managed to stay awake, but it wasn't easy.

After class Cindy approached Mrs. Lattner's desk, feeling doomed. The teacher was putting her papers into her briefcase. "Cindy, what has been going on this week?" she asked. "I'm very concerned about your behavior in class. Usually you're one of my better students."

Cindy smiled back uncertainly. She felt bad about letting the teacher down. "Nothing's wrong," she said. "I just have a lot to do at home."

"Well, don't lose sight of your priorities," Mrs. Lattner said. "Schoolwork should be number one for you now."

Wasn't that what Ashleigh had said, too? Cindy felt a flicker of irritation. Riding was more important to her than school—why couldn't anyone understand that? "I'll do better tomorrow," Cindy mumbled.

"I hope so." Mrs. Lattner snapped her briefcase shut.

Phew—I don't have detention! Cindy thought as she followed the teacher out of the classroom. *That could have been a lot worse.*

Cindy stood outside the classroom, feeling tired and overwhelmed. She tried not to think about how many classes she still had to get through that day. Did she have homework in any of them? She couldn't remember.

"Cindy!" Max called behind her.

"What?" Cindy shifted her books to one arm and rubbed her eyes with her free hand.

Max leaned on the lockers next to her. "I just wondered what's going on with you."

Max's question made her feel more aggravated.

Why did she have to constantly explain herself to everybody?

Cindy tried to get a grip on her temper. She knew it wasn't Max's fault that she was feeling tired and stressed. "Nothing's going on except that I'm preparing for my first race," she said shortly. "I've only got a week and a half left. I just don't have time to do anything but ride."

Max started to walk away. "Well, don't let me keep you," he said. "I guess I'll see you after the race."

Cindy grabbed his arm, pulling him back toward her. "Max, I can tell that you're annoyed. But right now, riding has to come first," she stated firmly. "I'm going to be a jockey. That takes a lot of dedication."

Max ran a hand through his hair and shrugged.

"Please don't fight with me now, Max," Cindy pleaded. "I'm just so busy and tired. It's almost impossible to handle both school and riding."

Max sighed. "All right," he said. "Maybe we can do something this weekend."

"Maybe," Cindy told him.

"I gotta go to class—I'll see you later," Max said as he turned to walk away.

"Bye." Cindy watched Max walk down the hall. She was glad that he seemed to understand. And the weekend was still days away. She might have more time . . . or she'd have to put Max off again.

"I won't worry about it yet," Cindy muttered to herself as she trudged off to gym class.

"You're not riding today, Cindy," Ian said on Friday morning as he walked up to Cindy in the training barn. He had returned to Whitebrook from Gulfstream the night before.

"I'm not?" Cindy dropped her hand from Honor's halter, feeling a quick blaze of anger. Being so tired was definitely shortening her temper. "But I have to!"

"Cindy, you've got the blackest rings around your eyes I've ever seen," her dad told her. "You're exhausting yourself, and that won't help you in your race. I don't want you to ride today. Go back up to the house and eat a decent breakfast, and do your schoolwork. Then tomorrow I want you to sleep in late and do something fun."

"I *am* having fun," Cindy protested, but her dad just frowned. She knew he wasn't crazy about her riding in races in the first place. If he thought she was making herself sick, he might forbid her to ride at all. "Okay, I won't exercise the horses tomorrow. I guess Ashleigh can ride Honor and Fleet Street. I'll do something *really* fun," she said glumly.

"Good." Ian nodded and strode briskly down the aisle.

Honor pushed her chest against her stall door and bobbed her head. The bay filly's eyes were bright with anticipation. She thought Cindy was about to take her out of her stall.

"I know," Cindy said. "That conversation didn't make any sense to you, either. I'm sorry, girl. You'll just have to stand there until Ashleigh gets around to you." Again Cindy felt a jolt of anger and frustration. Nobody told Ashleigh when to ride. That was why Ashleigh was such a great jockey.

Cindy dragged herself back up to the house. A pelting sleet was falling, but she wanted more than anything not to go inside. *Why did Dad have to stop me now?* she thought. *I'm never going to be as good as Ashleigh if no one will let me work at it!*

The next morning at nine o'clock Cindy poured herself a glass of milk and sat down at the kitchen table. Everyone else was out at the track, working with the horses, except for Beth and Kevin. They went to a play group every Saturday morning.

"What am I supposed to do?" Cindy asked herself. Warm sunlight was streaming through the window, glinting off the last of the ice from the storm the day before. Cindy could see the mares and foals frolicking and basking in the paddocks. She couldn't imagine staying inside all day.

"I have to ride, but I have to do something fun, too, because Dad said so," Cindy muttered, getting up to put a bagel in the toaster. "So how do I work that?"

She stepped up to the window. Cindy could see the right edge of the training track in the distance. Ashleigh and Samantha trotted by on Fleet Street and Honor. *That should be me out there*, Cindy thought enviously.

Cindy's bagel popped up. "I know—Max and I could go for a trail ride!" She grabbed the portable phone from the counter and punched in Max's number.

"Hello?" Max answered.

"Hi, Max," she said. "It's Cindy."

"Cindy who?" Max asked.

Max sounded kind of mad. Cindy couldn't tell if he was joking or not. "How many Cindys do you know?" she teased.

"Just one, but I thought you'd disappeared."

"No, I'm still here." *It's a good thing I called him*, Cindy thought. "Do you want to come over and go riding or something?" she asked.

"Wow. You're taking time out of your busy schedule for me?" Max asked sarcastically.

"Come on, Max." Cindy laughed. "Give me a break. You know how important my first race is to me."

Max was silent for a second. "All right. I guess we have to go riding—you don't want to do anything else. At least I'll get to see you."

Cindy smiled to herself. "Good. So, do you need to ask your mom to bring you over?"

"You *are* out of it," Max said. "Don't you remember that I can drive now?"

"Oh, yeah." Cindy paused. She did remember something about Max getting his license a couple of weeks ago—it had been a big deal for him. Cindy realized that she had never even congratulated him. "I'm sorry I'm so out of it, Max. But we'll catch up when you get here. I'll see you in a bit."

"Yeah, I'll be over soon," Max said. Cindy hung up the phone.

She hummed to herself as she went upstairs to brush her long blond hair. Gazing in the bathroom mirror, she had to admit that even one good night's sleep had worked wonders on her looks. The rings around her eyes were almost gone, and her complexion looked clear and healthy. Her hair was bright and shining.

I hope Max will think I look good, she said to herself. Cindy smiled shyly into the mirror, remembering how much she had enjoyed kissing him.

"He hasn't kissed me in a long time," she murmured. "Not since the big Christmas party at Ashleigh and Mike's house, and that was over a month ago. I really haven't seen much of him since then."

She heard a knock. "Coming!" Cindy rushed down the stairs and opened the door.

Max was leaning against the doorjamb. Cindy smiled up at him. Sometime in the past year Max had shot up to five-foot ten.

Max raised an eyebrow. "Ready to ride?"

"You bet!" Cindy impulsively kissed Max on the cheek and ran out the door past him, grabbing her jean jacket on the way.

"Hey, come back here!" Max called.

"No, you come out here!" Cindy twirled in a circle, letting the cool, fresh air slip through her fingers. "I've been dying to get outside," she called back to Max as she ran ahead.

He hurried to catch up to her, taking her hand in his when he reached her. Cindy liked the comfortable feel of holding his hand. She stopped walking and looked up at him again.

"It's good to see you," Max said warmly. "I mean, outside of school."

"I know what you mean. It's good to see you, too." Cindy smiled. She had forgotten how much she enjoyed being with him. She started walking again, this time more slowly, with Max's hand in hers.

"I'm really getting psyched for Donn day," Cindy told him, breathing in the crisp air. "And not just because of my race. All the Whitebrook horses are doing so well this year. Limitless Time just won another stakes at Gulfstream—the Broward Handicap, at a mile and a sixteenth."

"You already told me that," Max said impatiently, letting go of her hand.

"I did?" Cindy looked at him in surprise. She'd thought she just told Heather.

"Yes." He paused and sighed audibly. "But I understand that you're excited—Limitless is hitting the big time."

"Looks that way." Cindy stopped and gazed at the paddocks. Almost all the horses were outside, enjoying the pretty day. In the front paddock the seven yearling fillies were chasing one another in a game of tag. Glory's Joy seemed to be It. The dark gray filly was charging first at one yearling, then the next, thundering across the paddock for the sheer joy of running.

Cindy smiled. She was sure Glory's first filly would make them all proud at the track.

Whitebrook's six stallions were grazing in separate paddocks. Glory and Pride were in the paddocks closest to Cindy. Glory's dappled coat glittered silver in the sun, and Pride was a bright flame of chestnut. "What gorgeous guys," Cindy said to Max. She always thought that about the beautiful stallions, no matter how many times a day she saw them.

Max nodded, but he wasn't looking at Glory and Pride. Max seemed to be watching the exercise horses in the paddock right in front of them.

Glory flung up his head and whinnied when he saw Cindy. A moment later Pride echoed the greeting.

"Which horses do you want to take out?" Max asked.

Cindy thought a minute. "I hadn't really decided," she said.

"How about we go for a quiet ride and take Spirit and Chips?" Max asked, naming two of the exercise horses.

"Do you really want to?" Cindy asked in surprise. The racehorses had already gone back to the barn for the day, and so Cindy hadn't planned to ride Honor. But she wanted to take out a lively horse, like Glory or Pride. She'd hoped to get a workout for herself out of the trail ride, even if she wasn't riding on the track.

"Yeah, let's take the tamer guys," Max said firmly.

"Okay." Cindy didn't want to start a fight. *This might be my only chance to spend time with Max for a while*, she told herself as she followed Max to the geldings' paddock.

In the barn she tacked up Chips, a gentle Appaloosa. Chips dropped his head and half closed his eyes while Cindy checked the saddle girth. He seemed almost asleep. *This isn't going to be much fun,* she thought glumly. *I wonder why Max wants to go for an easy ride.* Max was a bold, talented rider. Usually they had a lot of fun on fast, hard rides.

Max already had Spirit ready and was waiting near the barn door. "Well, let's go," Cindy said, trying to sound enthusiastic. She tugged on Chips's reins, and the Appaloosa ambled after her.

Cindy and Max mounted the horses, then walked them across the stable yard to the trail that led to the woods. Cindy tried to touch up Chips with her heels, but the Appaloosa would have none of it. He walked faster for a stride or two, then dropped back into a leisurely stroll. "I guess that's the kind of ride this is," Cindy muttered. "But just don't walk so slow you stop dead, Chips."

Max had overheard. He laughed. "Hey, we can go faster in my car if you want," he said. "You've never even driven with me."

"That's true. So, are you a good driver?" Cindy wasn't too crazy about cars, but it *was* cool that he could drive anywhere now.

"The best," Max told her. "I love having my license."

"It must be great." Cindy looked over and smiled at him. "Now you don't have to ask your mom to drive you every time you want to go somewhere." It suddenly struck her how much independence Max had now.

"Exactly," Max responded. "And we can go anywhere, too. Maybe we'll go for a drive some time this weekend."

"That *would* be fun. We could go—" Cindy stopped talking to lean over Chips's neck as they passed under a branch. Max ducked, too.

Spirit sidled over to his paddock friend, Chips. Cindy sat up straight again and found herself looking right into Max's green eyes. "So we could go—" she began to murmur, but suddenly she had forgotten what she was about to say.

Max leaned over in the saddle and brushed her lips with his. Cindy closed her eyes briefly, savoring the softness of his kiss. When she opened them, the light seemed brighter and the outline of the bare gray trees was sharp against the crisp blue sky.

"This is why I wanted to go for a quiet ride," Max said softly. "I thought it might be nice for a change."

"It is." Cindy had spent a lot of time outside with the horses recently, but as she looked around the tranquil surroundings, she realized that it had been a long time since she really enjoyed nature and the pure joy of riding. She didn't even mind Chips's slow pace anymore—it was kind of relaxing. "We should do this more often," Cindy said.

"Yeah, we should." Max sounded surprised. He paused for a moment and then added, "How about tomorrow?"

Tomorrow? Cindy sat back in the saddle and thought about this for a moment. Then she suddenly panicked—she had no business making plans when this was her only day off. *My race is only a week away, and I'm making plans to go on drives and trail rides with Max? I can't get distracted like this if I'm going to be a top jockey,* she scolded herself.

"Cindy, are you there?" Max was still waiting for an answer.

"Hmm?" Cindy was pulled out of her thoughts. "Oh, yeah. Look, I really can't make any more plans this weekend, with my race in just one week."

"What about the skating party?" he said. "It's coming up pretty soon. I wanted to ask you—"

"I haven't thought much about it," Cindy cut in, all of a sudden feeling overwhelmed. *You should only be thinking about riding—no social distractions,* she reminded herself. "Honestly, all I can really afford to think about is my race." Cindy was suddenly so preoccupied with her upcoming race she didn't realize that Max hadn't responded. There was so much to prepare for—and look forward to. "The Dubai World Cup is coming up, too!" she continued, barely able to contain her excitement. "In less than two months I'll be in Arabia!"

Max was silent for a moment. "Sounds fun," he said finally. "I'm sure it'll be more fun than anything we could do in Kentucky."

"That's not what I meant," Cindy told him. "Besides, there are races here. They're already running at Turfway Park, and pretty soon the spring meets will start at Keeneland and Churchill Downs."

"I know, I know." Max sounded exasperated. He turned Spirit on the trail. "We gotta go back. I have to get home and help my mom."

"How come?" Cindy felt a quick rush of disappointment that their ride would be so short. Was Max mad at her?

"One of her veterinary assistants had a death in the family," Max said shortly. "He's out till next week."

"Oh." *Max already told me that*, Cindy reminded herself. "Well, if you really have to go, we'd better head back," she said slowly.

"Yeah, I do." Max trotted Spirit back down the trail.

Now he wants to ride fast, Cindy thought. As she watched him ride away, she couldn't help admiring his perfect form on a horse. Back straight and heels down, Max could sit motionless to a trot. He was an incredible horseman.

With a short whinny Chips trotted after Spirit. "You're finally awake. Just in time to run back to the barn," Cindy said. "You and Max," she added under her breath. Cindy knew she wasn't being fair, but she couldn't help wishing Max didn't have to go so soon. She was just starting to enjoy herself, and today was her one day off. But he had already dismounted at the barn.

Cindy caught up to him and dismounted also. "So maybe we'll go for that drive one day," she said as she walked with him toward his car.

Max sighed. "Sure, Cindy. Just let me know when you have time."

"Okay," Cindy said quietly. Truthfully, she didn't know when that would be.

Max kissed her cheek. "I guess I'll see you Monday," he told her. Then he got into his car.

"Bye," she said. *It was good to spend time with Max,* Cindy thought as she watched him drive away. *So why do I feel so lonely?*

6

A WEEK LATER, ON DONN SATURDAY AT GULFSTREAM, CINDY followed Ashleigh to the jockeys' room to change into her racing silks. "How are you feeling?" Ashleigh asked as they went inside.

"Fine," Cindy said, sinking onto a bench and dropping her duffel bag by her feet. She knew that was probably the biggest lie she'd ever told. Cindy was a bas-ket- case, and her stomach was turning around in knots.

She glanced around the jockeys' room, not believing that she was actually there. It was an ordinary room, with lockers lining the white-painted walls, rows of benches for the jockeys to sit on, a shower, and a TV that was running simulcast races from another track. But the room was bustling with activity as the other jockeys prepared for the race—the race that Cindy was actually going to be riding in herself. Just thinking about it made her heart beat faster.

What's the matter with me? Cindy thought. *I wasn't worried the past few days when I was riding Black Reason on the track.*

On Wednesday afternoon she had arrived in Miami and gone straight from the airport to Whitebrook's shed row. Cindy had spent the rest of the day getting reacquainted with the horses, the way she always did. Black Reason, Champion, and Limitless had all seemed happy to see her. She had talked to them, groomed them, and fed them treats. Ashleigh had good reports of their workouts.

The next morning Cindy had taken Black Reason out to the track for a gallop. For a moment she'd felt a flutter of nervousness. Cindy realized that her riding was for real now, not just practice at Whitebrook. But she had reminded herself just to pay attention to her horse and to what she was doing. The black colt had gone well for her.

Maybe I'll feel fine when I get out on the track again, Cindy tried to reassure herself. *If I can block out all of this racing excitement.*

As Cindy sat there processing everything, many of the other jockeys had left the room, and now it seemed deserted. Cindy slowly reached for her duffel bag, opened it, and drew out her brand-new racing silks, in the sky blue and white colors of Whitebrook. The material was soft but strong. She ran her fingers over it, hoping the beautiful outfit would bring her luck, the way Ashleigh's had.

"I'm not going to change yet, since the Donn goes off at the end of the day," Ashleigh said. "I just thought I'd keep you company."

Cindy nodded and set down her silks, still in awe that they were actually hers. "Thanks."

On the other side of the room a petite redheaded woman walked out of the shower room, toweling her hair.

"Sally Mitchell, I'd like you to meet Cindy McLean," Ashleigh introduced them. "Sally is a regular jock at Gulfstream. Cindy's riding before the stewards today in the six-furlong allowance race."

"Nice to meet you, Cindy." Sally smiled. "I just rode in the first race on the card, and I'm riding in your race, too. I'll be up on Sans Lyon."

Cindy wiped her sweating palm on her jeans before she shook hands with Sally. Sally's grip was firm and dry. *How can she and Ashleigh be so calm about riding in races?* she wondered.

"You'd better get changed, Cindy," Ashleigh said. "I'll be back in a couple of minutes."

Cindy fought the urge to beg Ashleigh to stay. Summoning every bit of her courage, she unzipped her jacket and reached for her silks. "I just have to make everyone proud of me today," she murmured.

"Your first race, huh?" said Sally Mitchell.

Cindy started. She had forgotten that Sally was in the room. "Yes," she said. "I'm riding Black Reason."

Sally nodded. "He's a nice horse," she said. "I saw him run last fall at Belmont with Ashleigh up."

With Ashleigh up. Cindy felt her stomach turn over. Would she be a letdown? "I've exercise-ridden Black Reason at Whitebrook," she said. "Just never in a race."

"Well, no matter what happens, you'll remember your first race for the rest of your life," Sally said wryly. "I fell off at the gate."

I didn't need to hear that. With trembling fingers Cindy drew her top over her head. Somehow she managed to get dressed.

Ashleigh walked back in the jockeys' room. "Look in the mirror," she said.

"Do I look all right?" Cindy got up and stepped over to the mirror. "Wow!" She grinned. Looking back at her she saw a smart, professional jockey. Cindy's confidence returned in a rush. *What am I so nervous for, anyway?* she thought. *I'm well prepared for the race. I've got a lot of experience around racehorses, and I worked so hard last week.*

"Ready?" Ashleigh asked.

Cindy drew in a deep breath. "Yup." She nodded. She was eager to get out there and prove herself.

The Florida day was sunny and mild. Cindy relished the warmth of the sun beating down on her neck and shoulders as she followed Ashleigh to the walking ring. A large crowd had gathered to watch the horses, and Cindy was aware of the noise in a way she never had been before. Before, she had been part of the crowd making the noise. Now she felt like an actor on a stage, and all of that cheering and yelling was directed at her.

"Good luck." Sally Mitchell walked past her on Sans Lyon and gave her a thumbs-up.

"Thanks." Cindy smiled, but she felt her fears start up again. She had imagined this race so many times, but jockeys like Sally and Ashleigh had ridden in dozens of races. Sally looked so relaxed and competent. *I'm really going to have to ride well to beat her,* Cindy thought. *Can I do it?*

In a blur Cindy mounted Black Reason with a leg up from Len. She saw her dad's worried face and the rest of her family waving as she rode off toward the tunnel to the track with an escort pony, but she didn't have time to think about them now.

On the track Cindy walked and trotted Black Reason with the other horses in the post parade. "You're a good boy, aren't you?" Cindy asked. Her voice sounded quavery to her own ears. "We'll do okay out there."

The black colt snorted softly as Cindy turned him

back toward the gate. He seemed to be saying he would try his best.

"You look just perfect," Cindy whispered. The black colt's sleek coat flashed in the sun, and his short, mincing steps at the trot belied the hidden power of his toned muscles. He was highly conditioned. Of course Ashleigh had ridden him at the track while Cindy was in school. *Black Reason will go well for you, too,* Cindy told herself. *He always has.*

The assistant starter led Black Reason into the five slot of the gate. Cindy positioned herself carefully over the colt's withers and wrapped her hands in his thick mane. The four horse, a gray California colt named Wright's Might, was kicking the gate next to them.

Don't pay attention to him, Cindy ordered herself, staring straight ahead at the metal bars of the gate. She could hear the six horse loading next to them. That would be Sally Mitchell on Sans Lyon, a Florida bred. Or was it Heart of Mine, a black colt from Kentucky? There was Day's End, a speedball, also from Florida. What post position had he drawn? Cindy had read every bit of information about the field in the racing papers, but she couldn't remember much of it now. At that moment, she felt like she couldn't remember much of anything. She was all nerves.

Only seconds had gone by, but Cindy felt as if she'd been in the tight confines of the gate for hours.

Sweat trickled from her forehead. She didn't dare loosen her grip on the reins to wipe it off. She tried to concentrate only on her horse.

Black Reason shifted gently and pricked his ears. "Are you ready?" Cindy whispered.

"The horses are in the gate," the announcer called as the ten horse loaded. Cindy stiffened, feeling alert in every nerve. The bell clanged and the gates slammed open. "And they're off!"

Black Reason broke cleanly out of the gate, just the way Cindy had practiced with him so many times. But Day's End and Wright's Might were away faster and had beaten them to the rail!

Where did they come from—where do I go? Cindy thought desperately. The thunder of hooves was deafening. To her inside the two speed horses fought for the lead. To the outside the seven other horses in the race jockeyed for position. The jumble of bodies, moving at high speed, was overwhelming.

Suddenly Heart of Mine rushed by Cindy and Black Reason, going four wide around the far turn to challenge for the lead. Big clods of stinging dirt flew into Cindy's face.

What now? she thought frantically. Black Reason swayed to the inside to avoid Fire in the Hole, another of the Florida-bred horses, and Cindy almost lost her seat. *I can't tell what all of those horses are going to do,* she thought. *I know my horse, but that doesn't help!*

The field roared into the far turn. "And it's Heart of Mine on the lead," she heard the announcer call. "Back one to Day's End and Wright's Might, battling for second. Black Reason is running in fourth, in the clear and on the outside. . . ."

Don't give up! Cindy ordered herself. *Fourth isn't last—you're in good position. But you've got to make a move!*

Suddenly Cindy saw that Day's End and Wright's Might were bearing out on the turn. A hole had opened up on the rail—not much, but just enough for a horse to get through.

"Trust yourself—go for it!" Cindy whispered. But before she could cue Black Reason, Sally Mitchell shot through on Sans Lyon, cutting Cindy off. More dirt hit Cindy's face.

Cindy instantly realized that dirt was the least of her problems. Black Reason was about to run up on the heels of Sans Lyon! Cindy was forced to check her colt hard.

Black Reason threw up his head in protest, but he dropped his pace. *This is not good,* Cindy thought rapidly. *I've really blown it!*

"And at the top of the stretch it's Sans Lyon taking the lead in a daring move, charging through on the inside," she heard the announcer say. "Back one to Day's End and Wright's Might. Black Reason is in fourth, trapped behind horses. Heart of Mine is backing up in fifth. . . ."

Black Reason was pounding across the track, his strides steady and ground eating. The colt's ears flicked back, waiting for Cindy's instructions. He hadn't given up on her or the race!

We're not out of this yet, Cindy thought with fresh determination. *If we can't go between horses, we'll go around!*

She pulled Black Reason's head firmly to the outside and pressed her hands into his neck. The black colt responded with a surge of speed, drawing even with Day's End. Cindy saw the other jockey go for his whip, but Black Reason pulled ahead of the other black colt. "Go after Wright's Might next, boy!" she whispered hoarsely.

But before she knew it the wire was flashing overhead. The race was over, and she had lost.

"Sans Lyon wins it, with Wright's Might up for the place," the announcer called. "Strong late rally by Black Reason in third."

Cindy could hardly believe her ears. As if in a dream she galloped out Black Reason another furlong, then circled the colt to go back to the gap. "I was so sure we'd win, boy," she whispered. "What happened to me out there?"

The black colt tipped back his ears and turned his head so that he could watch her with one dark eye. Even though they'd lost, he still trusted her to tell him what to do. *I don't deserve his trust*, Cindy said to herself miserably. *There was just so much to do out there!*

At the gap Len stepped forward quickly to meet them. "I've got him, Cindy," Len said gently, taking the reins out of her hands. "You did just fine."

"No, I didn't—I let down Black Reason, and everybody at Whitebrook, and myself!" Cindy cried.

"Cindy, the steward found your performance satisfactory, so you can ride in other races," Ashleigh said. "You did some things right. You just let the tension get to you."

Cindy dismounted and pressed her face against Black Reason's neck.

"Don't worry, honey," Ian added. "You know you can't win them all."

"But I haven't won any!" Cindy fought back tears. "And I probably never will!"

"Look, Cindy, I lost my first race," Ashleigh pointed out. "I would watch the video we made of this race, learn from it, and move on."

"But you didn't make a mistake like I did." Cindy bit her lip, trying to stop her tears from falling.

"It doesn't matter," Ashleigh began. "Every race is different—"

"It does matter!" Cindy cried, rubbing her cheek against Black Reason's silken neck. Couldn't Ashleigh understand why she was so upset?

"Come on, Cindy—calm down and take a second to collect yourself," Samantha said gently. "You don't want to cry in front of all these people. Let's get Black Reason back to the barn and take care of him."

"I know, I know." Cindy drew in a deep breath and rubbed her eyes dry with her fists. "I'm okay. I've got to be professional."

"That's the spirit," Ian said approvingly.

Cindy squared her shoulders. "I'm going to congratulate Sally Mitchell," she said.

"Good idea." Ashleigh's expression was sympathetic, but that didn't make Cindy feel any better. She felt so bad about the race, she could hardly make her expression pleasant.

Cindy pushed through the crowd toward Sally. The older jockey had just stepped out of the winner's circle. She and her horse were surrounded by reporters and well-wishers.

"Great ride," Cindy said. "Congratulations."

Sally smiled. "Thanks. Listen, Cindy, you rode pretty well. . . ."

Cindy turned on her heel before Sally could say anything more. Cindy knew Sally was trying to be nice, but she couldn't bear it. *I don't want to ride pretty well*, she thought. *I thought I was a great rider until today!*

"Cindy!" Beth waved from the edge of the crowd. "Let's go back to the motel and get washed up," she said calmly, putting an arm around Cindy's shoulders. "We still have time to get back here before the Donn."

She kissed the top of Cindy's head. "Don't look so down, honey. Isn't riding in a race at a big track like Gulfstream wonderful no matter what happens?"

Cindy eased out of Beth's embrace. *I just don't want any more sympathy from anyone right now,* she thought. She knew that her mother was trying to comfort her, but she was afraid that if her family said one more nice word, she would burst into a flood of frustrated tears. She wanted to pretend that she agreed with them—that this was just one loss, and that she was lucky to be here at all. But underneath, Cindy's heart was breaking.

"I should go to the jockeys' room to change," she told Beth. "Then I'll go back to the barn and help Len with Champion." Cindy wasn't looking forward to the conversation with the other riders in the jockeys' room, but she knew she should face them.

I bet I would have won on a superhorse like Champion, she thought as she wove through the crowd toward the jockeys' room. *But maybe I'm making excuses. I lost my concentration in the race, and that's because I didn't work hard enough. I wish I didn't have stupid school— then I could have been here riding Black Reason, where I belong.*

In the walking ring grooms and trainers circled the horses for the next race. Cindy stopped to look, letting the streams of people pass her on all sides. No one paid the least bit of attention to her.

84

"I sure can't ask to ride Champion in Dubai after this," she murmured. "I just have to do better."

A magnificent bay in the walking ring whinnied sharply and reared. The groom urged the colt back down on all fours. But his eyes still gleamed, and he pranced eagerly in place.

He wants like crazy to get out on the track, Cindy realized. *And so do I!*

"Only next time I'll do things differently," Cindy told herself. "I won't lose my focus, no matter what. I'll cut out all my after-school activities and I won't waste any time with my friends. I won't even study except in study hall. I'm going to win my next race and prove to Ashleigh I should ride Champion in the Dubai World Cup! It's what I want more than anything."

7

ON MONDAY AT SCHOOL CINDY WALKED SLOWLY DOWN THE hall toward her locker, wishing she were anywhere but where she was. The only reason that she was glad to be in school was because she'd see Max. She hadn't had a chance to tell him about the disaster at Gulfstream yet. For some reason he hadn't been in first-period English. Cindy's steps quickened as she approached her locker, which was close to Max's. Usually she could catch him there before her math class. She realized that after losing at Gulfstream, talking to Max was one of the only things that would make her happy.

Cindy's loss at Gulfstream hadn't ended with her

own race. That afternoon Ashleigh had ridden Champion to a four-length victory in the Donn Handicap, and Ashleigh and Champion were the talk of the racing world. Cindy was glad for Champion, but she just couldn't find it in herself to be happy for Ashleigh. Ashleigh had so many victories and got so much attention already. Cindy hadn't even won a race.

Cindy spun the combination lock on her locker and looked impatiently down the hall. Max had just turned the corner. "Max!" Cindy started to call, then she saw that he wasn't alone. Laura was walking next to him, talking animatedly about something. Cindy felt a jolt of disappointment.

Max and Laura hadn't seen her yet. *Aren't they walking kind of close together?* Cindy wondered.

She flushed, realizing that she was jealous, and turned toward her locker to take out her math book.

"Hey, Cindy," Max said.

With a big smile Cindy turned to greet him—and saw Laura standing right beside him. "Oh . . . hi," she said flatly.

Laura smiled and touched Max's arm. "I'll see you later, Max," she said. "Bye, Cindy."

"Bye," Cindy responded, wondering when Max and Laura became so close. "So, what's up? You weren't in English," she said to Max.

"I had a doctor's appointment," he explained. "But I'm fine. How did it go?" Max asked.

"Not great," Cindy admitted, but she was already feeling better talking to him. "I only came in third."

"I figured you'd have called if you'd won," Max said. "But third isn't bad for your first race. What happened?"

Max's tone was supportive. Relieved, she rapidly filled him in on the race and what Ashleigh had said about it.

Max listened intently. "You should listen to Ashleigh," he told her. "I think you're stressed out. You put so much pressure on yourself—it's no wonder you couldn't react as quickly as you'd have liked. You need a clear head to ride."

He's just agreeing with Ashleigh? Cindy thought in dismay.

"Look, you're a great rider," Max continued. "Even the greatest jockeys lose races. Just because you lost one race, for whatever reason, doesn't mean you don't have talent." Max picked up her hand and squeezed it reassuringly.

Cindy didn't agree with everything he had said—she still felt that she had to work harder—but the warmth of his hand and smile helped to put her problem into perspective. *Everything isn't over for me,* she thought. *I can still get out on the track and win.* She smiled back at Max. *And I still have Max. It feels so good to talk to him.*

"So what have you been doing while I was gone?" Cindy asked.

Max let go of her hand and stepped to his locker to

get his books. "Not much," he said over his shoulder. "We had a meeting on Friday about the skating party."

The skating party! Cindy had forgotten all about it. The bell rang for classes, and a crowd of students swept by them. "Do you have a date?" Cindy asked, half joking. She was sure Max had already been planning to go with her.

Max looked surprised, then embarrassed. "I thought you didn't want to go," he said. "So I asked Laura."

Cindy felt like she'd just been slapped across the face. *He asked Laura?* She could hardly believe it was true. An image of Laura's pretty face flashed into her mind . . . and of Max bending his head close to Laura's as they walked down the hall together.

"Oh . . . um, okay," she finally said awkwardly. The words echoed strangely in her ears and she felt her cheeks burning red. "I guess that's that. . . . I'll see you later." Cindy turned on her heel and desperately pushed through the crowded hallway. She wasn't sure if she was going to cry or faint or scream, but she knew she just had to get away from Max.

"Wait, Cindy—" he called after her.

"It's time for class!" Cindy dodged into her math class and found her seat, almost blinded by tears. Mr. Wilshire, her math teacher, was already writing problems on the blackboard.

Cindy opened her math book. *I just won't think about what happened,* she told herself. *I can't stand it.*

But she couldn't think of anything else. The numbers on the page swam before her eyes. She dropped her head to hide her tears. *How could I not see I was losing him?* she wondered miserably. *This is just like the race—I thought nothing could go wrong there, either. And I lost. Now my whole life is messed up.*

Cindy looked up at the blackboard, but she didn't see any math equations. She was thinking about when she first met Max, back in sixth grade, when he'd teased her and everyone said he had a crush on her. She thought about when he raced Spirit across the meadows of Whitebrook, riding hard and wild. And her heart breaking, Cindy remembered the soft look in his eyes as he bent his head toward hers for her first kiss, last year after the ninth-grade dance.

Cindy buried her head in her hands. *I blew it royally*, she realized. *I totally took Max for granted, and now he's with Laura. But what can I do? I can't stop spending every possible second with the horses, not after what happened at Gulfstream. I'll lose him forever. . . .*

Cindy dropped her head on her desk and closed her eyes.

"Cindy, do you want to go to the nurse's office?" Mr. Wilshire asked gently.

"No, I'm fine." Cindy sat up straight. *I'm not going to act like my heart is breaking even if it is*, she thought. *I have some pride!*

To make matters worse, after class she noticed that the entire school was festooned with a love theme. Red, white, and pink paper hearts and smiling Cupids shooting arrows hung all over the walls. BE MINE, VALENTINE, said a huge heart directly over the door of Cindy's history class.

"Happy Valentine's Day, Cindy!" said Mr. Alton, her history teacher, as he walked around her into the classroom. Cindy stared after him stupidly.

Oh, no, it's Valentine's Day! she realized in dismay. *I forgot about that, too. Great timing.*

She sank into her chair, realizing that this day had hit a new low. She wondered what everyone would think if she tore down all the Cupids and hearts.

Cindy passed the rest of the school day in utter misery. Several of her teachers called on her in class, but she couldn't put together any answers. After what seemed like a century, the final-period bell rang. Cindy jumped to her feet and rushed to the door of her science class.

"What's with you, Cindy?" Melissa asked as she walked out of the classroom with her. "You were a total space cadet in there."

"Nothing." Cindy wondered if Melissa really did know what was wrong. She and Laura were best friends.

Cindy rushed down the hall to get to the bus, trying not to look up at the colorful decorations that seemed to mock her from every wall. "Thank goodness this day is over," she murmured. "I just want to go home and get in bed."

Max and Laura were walking toward her. "Not them," Cindy muttered under her breath. "I can't take this." But before she could run away, she saw that Max was holding a bouquet of red roses. As Cindy watched he handed the roses to Laura. "I don't believe it!" Cindy gasped. Fresh tears sprang to her eyes and her heart felt like it was breaking all over again. She ran outside before Max could see her.

Cindy hardly knew how she got on the bus. *Why did I have to see Max give Laura those flowers?* she asked herself, almost sobbing as she made her way down the aisle of the bus. *It's bad enough that he doesn't care about me. But that was like rubbing salt in my wounds.*

Heather was already sitting at the back of the bus. *At least I can talk to Heather about all this,* Cindy thought. That was a tiny bit of comfort.

"Happy Valentine's Day," Heather greeted Cindy as she sat down beside her.

Cindy groaned. "No, it isn't! What's so happy about it?"

"Well, Doug and I are going out to dinner." Doug Mellinger and Heather spent time together the way Cindy and Max had. Heather hesitated. "That's all."

"Don't be afraid to tell me the details." Cindy looked out the window. The day was gray, and a pale

92

yellow, wintry sun hung low in the sky. "Just because I'm not going anywhere," she added.

"Hey, are you all right?" Heather asked, looking concerned. "Aren't you and Max going out tonight?"

"Nope." Cindy's chest squeezed painfully. "He didn't ask me. And . . ." Cindy couldn't bring herself to talk about Laura.

"You haven't been around much, Cindy," Heather pointed out. "I mean, when could Max have asked you to do anything? He may have thought you wouldn't even be back from Gulfstream by today."

"I know, I know. But I guess there's no changing things now. Max is gone." The bus was rolling through open countryside, and the Thoroughbreds in the fields were splashes of vibrant chestnut, black, and gray against the dark day. But for once Cindy couldn't enjoy the sight. She almost thought she might be sick.

"What do you mean, Max is gone?" Heather said in surprise.

"Max is seeing Laura," Cindy said heavily, still almost not believing it. She wished Heather would just leave it at that. What else was there to say?

"Really? That's news to me," Heather stared at her. "Are you sure?"

"About five minutes ago Max gave Laura a bouquet of red roses," Cindy said angrily. Her throat was constricted so much, she could hardly breathe out the words.

Heather looked stunned. "Wow. That is bad news."

"So I'm sure they're going out tonight," Cindy finished. "Can we just drop the subject?"

Heather was silent for a moment. "You know, Cindy, Max really likes you—"

"*Liked* me, you mean," Cindy interrupted. "I said I didn't want to talk about it."

Heather plowed on. "But you never paid any attention to him. You never put any effort into the relationship—"

"I realize that now," Cindy cried, "but it's too late. Listen, it's just making me more upset to talk about it."

"Sorry." Heather patted her shoulder. "I just wouldn't give up on Max yet."

"Okay, okay." Cindy buried her head in her hands. *I guess we all agree—I made a thousand mistakes with Max*, she thought. "So where are you and Doug going to dinner?" she asked, trying to change the subject.

"Just Dante's," Heather replied, naming a popular Italian restaurant. She smiled.

"Call me after and tell me how it went." Even though Cindy was having a horrible Valentine's Day herself, she still wanted her friend to be happy.

"I will," Heather said gently.

She knows how bad I feel, Cindy thought. *It's nice to have sympathy—I guess.*

At Whitebrook, Cindy walked slowly up the driveway to her house. A blustery wind shook the bare trees and nipped Cindy's face. *I'm glad it's nasty out,* she thought, brushing her hair away from her damp cheeks. *Why should anything be good about this day?*

A shrill whinny from the front paddock interrupted her thoughts. Cindy recognized the filly's voice without looking. "Hi, Honor!" she called.

The gorgeous filly was trotting up and down the fence line, bobbing her head over the top board of the fence. Honor wore a warm, deep purple blanket. She looked like a royal princess. Cindy felt a quick, unexpected burst of joy.

"Hey, girl." Cindy stopped at the paddock and ran her fingers down Honor's silken neck. "How's your day been?"

Honor leaned forward against the boards. She seemed about to tell Cindy, but Fleet Street pushed by her. The black filly stuck her nose in between the boards, eagerly seeking a pat from Cindy.

Honor's ears flattened. She twisted her head, ready to take a bite out of Fleet Street.

"Oh, stop it, Honor," Cindy scolded. "See? I have two hands. I can pat both of you." Cindy patted Honor's perfect star and scratched Fleet Street's neck at the same time.

The bay filly settled down, but she still had her ears cocked slightly back. Seeming to take the hint,

Fleet Street stepped away from the fence and went back to grazing.

"You really are bossy, Honor," Cindy said, smiling. "I guess that's good—most of the time."

Honor tossed her pretty head and whinnied again.

"I get the message," Cindy told her. "Just let me get changed, then I'll take you out on the trails. That'll be good for both of us."

Feeling better, Cindy hurried up to the house. She kicked off her school shoes in the entryway and walked into the kitchen.

"Hi, sweetheart," Beth said. She and Kevin sat at the kitchen table, Beth drinking herbal tea and Kevin eating chocolate cookies. "Did you get any valentines?"

"No," Cindy said shortly. She saw the look of surprise on Beth's face. In an instant Cindy's bad mood returned. She headed for the stairs to her room, not wanting to explain about Max. *I wish this day were over*, she thought. *I wish I'd never heard of Valentine's Day!*

Cindy quickly changed into riding boots and jeans. The sooner she got back out with the horses, the better. *I think too much about my social life*, she told herself as she bounded back downstairs. *I should just work on my riding and not worry about Max. Nothing's going to change what happened with him, anyway.*

Cindy took two apples out of the refrigerator, one for herself and one for Honor. "See you later," she called to Beth. "I'm going to ride."

Beth laughed. "That's no surprise. Where are you going?"

"I guess on the trails." Cindy pulled her down jacket from the hook in the hall and tucked the apples in her pockets. "But I need someone to ride with."

"Sammy's still at school," Beth said, wiping chocolate from Kevin's mouth with a napkin.

The small red-haired boy grinned at Cindy. Despite her unhappiness, Cindy grinned back. Kevin really was irresistible. "Well, if I can't find anybody to ride with, I'll just fool around the stable yard with Honor or something," Cindy said as she opened the outside door.

The clouds were still hanging low as Cindy walked to the barn to get Honor's halter. The ground, wet and spongy from last night's snowfall, tugged at her boots.

"Hi, Cindy." Ashleigh walked out of the mares' barn, leading Wonder under tack. The mare was sixteen now, but the alert expression in her dark eyes was unchanged.

"May I ride with you?" Cindy asked. If she could watch Ashleigh ride, she might be able to pick up some tips.

Ashleigh nodded. "Yep. Actually I was waiting for you."

"Great!" Cindy whirled and rushed into the barn. "I'll be ready in a second—just let me get Honor!" she called back.

"I'll be here. Take it easy!" Ashleigh said with a laugh.

Cindy trotted Honor to the barn and brushed and tacked up the filly in record time. She wanted to get Ashleigh away from the farm before the phone rang or something else happened that would demand Ashleigh's attention.

Cindy quickly led Honor over to the mounting block and jumped into the saddle. The filly snorted excitedly, dancing on her black-stockinged legs.

"Let's go!" Ashleigh's hazel eyes sparkled.

"I'm ready." Cindy smiled, feeling much better herself.

She glanced over at Wonder as they walked the horses to the trails. The gorgeous chestnut mare stepped delicately along on the muddy path, clearly enjoying the outing. Honor pranced beside her, kicking up her heels just a bit with delight as a light shower of snow drifted off the trees, blanketing her in a cool curtain. Cindy grinned as she lost her balance a little. "Wild thing," she said affectionately, reaching to straighten Honor's black mane.

Cindy looked over to watch Ashleigh ride and saw that Ashleigh was watching her. "You really know how to handle Honor, Cindy," she said.

"Thanks." Cindy flushed with pleasure. She knew that no one was a better judge of horsemanship than Ashleigh.

"Do you want to ride Wonder?" Ashleigh asked after a moment.

"Sure!" Cindy was startled. No one but Ashleigh ever rode Wonder—she was Ashleigh's special horse. *Maybe Ashleigh hasn't lost all her confidence in me since I lost my race*, Cindy thought.

Cindy dismounted from Honor and traded reins with Ashleigh. Then Cindy lowered the stirrup on Wonder's saddle so that she could get on the mare.

Wonder swung her hindquarters away a little as Cindy mounted. The sensitive mare was clearly uneasy about her new rider.

"It's okay," Cindy soothed. "It's just me, Wonder. We've known each other for ages."

The mare seemed to remember. She settled down into a spirited walk, tossing her head a little.

Cindy shook back her hair, enjoying the cool bite of the wind on her face and the supple creak of the saddle leather. Wonder's walk was as smooth as butter, and Cindy was thrilled to ride the famous Derby-winning mare. *This Valentine's Day is shaping up a little*, she thought.

At a fork in the path Cindy asked Wonder to turn toward the galloping lane. The mare hesitated, as if she had to think about what Cindy wanted for a second. Then she did what Cindy asked. *Wonder is completely Ashleigh's horse*, Cindy realized, feeling a sting of envy. She could tell that every movement of the mare was fine-tuned to Ashleigh to an amazing degree.

Cindy turned in the saddle to see how Ashleigh was doing with Honor. The bay filly, her coat gleaming against the gray-and-white wintry trees, was going well for the experienced jockey. The filly spooked a little for fun from a pile of snow, then dodged the other way from a suspicious clump of branches. Ashleigh calmly rode it all out, her feet and hands perfectly still.

Cindy's spirits sank again. *I ride Honor well, but Ashleigh's better*, she thought. *Even though I ride Honor a lot more than Ashleigh does.*

"Honor's going really well for you," Cindy said. She wanted to be fair. Ashleigh certainly gave her a lot of compliments.

Ashleigh smiled. "Thanks. But I think you do as well or better, Cindy. You're doing fine with Wonder, but it's the high-strung horses you seem to understand best. Like Champion and Honor." Ashleigh seemed deep in thought.

"Will Champion race again before Dubai?" Cindy asked.

"No, I don't think so," Ashleigh replied. "He doesn't need it."

Cindy nodded. "When do you want me to go back to Gulfstream?" she asked. "Can I exercise Champion before he leaves for Dubai?"

"Definitely," Ashleigh said. "But I have bigger plans for you. Are you ready to ride in another race?"

Cindy looked quickly over at her. Her spirits soared. "You bet!"

Ashleigh laughed. "I thought you'd say that. Let's enter you and Black Reason in another allowance race at seven furlongs, at the end of February. I think Black Reason is going to be a sprinter, and this race may tell us that for sure. You could go back to Gulfstream before that to work with Reason and Champion, too. I know you'll miss quite a bit of school, but Ian and Beth are going to talk to your teachers."

"Thanks, Ashleigh, for giving me another chance as a jockey!" Cindy grinned. Wonder sprang into a trot, sensing Cindy's excitement. Cindy heard Honor's quick trot as she increased her pace to keep up with the older horse.

"Well, that's not all I had in mind." Ashleigh hesitated. "You see, Limitless has been invited to run in the Dubai World Cup. He's a substitute for Rising Chief, who had to be scratched."

"Wow, that's great news!" Cindy said excitedly. She remembered how thrilled Ashleigh, Ian, and Mike had been that Champion was invited. This was a double honor.

"I think Limitless deserves it," Ashleigh said thoughtfully. "He hasn't gotten the attention he deserves because Champion's always grabbed the limelight.

But I think Limitless will give Champion a run for the wire."

"So who's going to ride Limitless, since you're riding Champion?" Cindy asked.

Ashleigh stopped Honor and looked directly at Cindy. "I am. You're going to ride Champion."

"What?" Cindy spluttered. She fell back in the saddle and almost tipped off backward. Wonder stopped walking to let her get her bearings. "I am? I mean, that's so great. I can't believe it—"

Ashleigh held up a hand. "Wait. You'll ride him *if* you put in a good ride in Black Reason's next allowance race and *if* Champion's workouts with you go well. Then you'll have earned your ticket to Dubai."

"Yes!" Cindy shouted jubilantly. Wonder started and jumped sideways. "Sorry, girl. But that's the most exciting news ever. Thanks so much, Ashleigh!"

"No need for thanks. I'm not doing this as a favor to you, although I'm happy to be giving you the opportunity," Ashleigh said, letting Honor walk on. "You've always had a special bond with Champion, and I really think he'll go best for you. He's going to have to make a real effort to win against the competition and on the sand surface in Dubai."

Cindy grinned. "I'll study up on the track over there. I'm sure Whitebrook's going to finish one-two in Dubai!"

"Don't get ahead of yourself," Ashleigh warned. "We're not going to walk away with this race. Most of the European and Asian horses entered in the Dubai World Cup are tough, but not a real threat. But guess who else is racing in Dubai?"

"I don't know." Cindy's mind was spinning at a million miles a second, trying to take in everything Ashleigh had said.

"Ben Cavell's Just Deserts."

"That's so great for Ben!" Cindy grinned broadly. Like Glory, Just Deserts was a grandson of the famous sire Just Victory. Cindy had met Just Deserts on a trip to Ben's farm in Virginia and had been impressed by the colt, then only a few months old. Ben had been Glory's first trainer and had later helped Cindy get Glory over the worst of his training problems.

"This is shaping up to be quite a race," Ashleigh said. She glanced at the sky. "Well, it's getting dark. We'd better take the horses back and get going on our evening chores."

"All right, sure." Cindy was so filled with energy, she thought she might burst.

Ashleigh turned Honor back toward the barn. "I'm going to trot Honor out a little. I'll see you in a bit."

Cindy watched Ashleigh ride off. She forced herself to sit quietly for a few moments in the darkening forest, letting all the good news sink in. "Wait a minute," she said softly. "If Whitebrook finishes one-two, who'll be two?"

Cindy shivered in the growing chill and damp of the forest. She had always hoped to be as good a jockey as Ashleigh. But for the first time Cindy realized that would mean beating Ashleigh in a race.

"Can I really do it?" she asked herself. "What do you think, Wonder?"

The beautiful mare stamped and strained her neck in the direction of Ashleigh and Honor. In the quickly falling night, Cindy could barely see them.

"You're right; it's time for dinner. And I guess you're the wrong horse to ask, anyway." Cindy let up on the reins a little. Wonder set off for home at a brisk walk.

But if I win the Dubai World Cup, I've got it made, Cindy thought. *Everyone will finally take me seriously as a jockey, and they'll stop telling me to devote my time to other things. I just have to beat Ashleigh—if that's possible.*

8

THE NEXT MORNING CINDY DRAGGED HERSELF AWAY FROM Glory's paddock. "If I don't change clothes in about one minute, I'm going to miss the bus," she reminded herself.

Cindy walked back to give Glory one last pat anyway. The silvery stallion was great company—and after what had happened yesterday with Max, she could hardly bear the thought of going to school.

Cindy dropped her head into her hands. "How can I face Max, Glory?" she asked. "Are he and Laura going to be holding hands right in front of me? I wish I could transfer to another school."

Glory bumped Cindy with his soft black muzzle

and shook his mane. "I know, you can't help me with this," Cindy said with a rueful smile. "But thanks for the support."

She walked away backward from the paddock, watching Glory gallop rapidly up and down the fence line. The big stallion gave a sharp snort of pleasure every time he turned to go in the other direction. *Well, at least one of us is going to have a good day*, she thought. *I wonder just how awful my day is going to be.*

"I'll drive you to school, Cindy," Beth said when Cindy opened the cottage door. "I think the bus is already gone."

"Thanks." Cindy was glad that she wouldn't have to talk to Heather on the bus. She hoped that Heather had had a wonderful time last night with Doug, but she really wasn't up to hearing all about Heather's dream dinner. And she didn't want to talk about Max, either. "This is sad," Cindy murmured as she jammed her schoolbooks into her backpack. "I've got such great news about the Dubai World Cup and my next race, but I don't want to go anywhere near my two best friends."

Beth dropped Cindy off at school, and she stood outside for several minutes, hopping from one foot to the other in the cold. Cindy hoped if she was late enough, she wouldn't run into Max and Laura. *I wish I could just stay outside all day*, she thought, squeezing

106

her fingers to warm them up. The day was chilly and gray.

Cindy shivered. *How am I going to get through English, sitting next to Max? It's going to be absolute torture. I guess I could cut.*

But Cindy knew that if she cut class, her parents would almost certainly find out. Then they wouldn't let her miss school to ride in races. No matter what, Cindy couldn't let that happen. With a heavy sigh she walked into the building.

Cindy slid into her seat in English class right after the bell rang. Max was already there, sitting next to her, but Cindy didn't give him so much as a glance.

"Hey, Cindy . . ." Max leaned toward her.

"Hi," Cindy said quickly. Then she pointed at Mrs. Lattner and shook her head. Max sat back.

He probably thinks I'm worried about getting detention, she thought. *He doesn't even know what's wrong!* For just a second Cindy glanced in Max's direction. *I sure wish I could tell him that I'm working toward racing in Dubai.*

The moment class was over, Cindy raced for the door. Luckily she got outside the classroom just ahead of a large group of students who blocked Max's path. "Made it," she said triumphantly, but her heart ached.

As she ran down the hall Cindy remembered the last time she'd avoided Max at school. A year ago he'd asked her to a dance for the first time. Cindy had refused to go, worried that he might think of her as his girlfriend. She hadn't thought that she was ready for that yet.

Now Max has asked Laura out, just when I was starting to think of him as my boyfriend, she thought. *We never made it official, but I didn't think that he'd ever start to go out with somebody else!*

Cindy glumly shoved her books into her gym locker. *I'll just work hard at school and with the horses,* she thought. *I don't have time for Max, anyway—Dubai is much too important.*

A couple of hours later, after fifth period, Heather flagged her down in the hall. "Cindy! I've been trying to find you all day! Where have you been?"

"Around," Cindy said defensively. She didn't want Heather to know that she'd hidden in different rest rooms in between all her classes to avoid Max. When the halls were empty, she'd run to class.

"I tried to call you last night, but the line was busy," Heather went on.

"I guess Sammy was talking on the phone to Tor." Cindy looked over Heather's shoulder to make sure Max wasn't in sight.

"I was wondering if I could come over for a trail ride after school," Heather said.

"Yeah, sure," Cindy mumbled. Was that Laura behind that group of laughing students? Cindy's hands began to shake.

"I'll meet you at the bus, okay?" Heather waved her hand in front of Cindy's face.

"Okay!" Cindy ducked into her science class. *Safe.* "Oh, how was your dinner?" she called back, but Heather was already gone.

Well, I'm sure I'll hear all about it later, Cindy thought. *At least somebody has a happy love life.*

"Okay, Cindy, what's going on with Max?" Heather asked when they got to Whitebrook after school that day. Cindy and Heather had stopped off for a snack at the cottage, then gone down to the training barn to get the horses ready for their trail ride. They had crosstied Honor and Chips and carried the horses' tack out of the tack room.

Heather had babbled about her great dinner with Doug the whole bus ride home. Cindy was relieved in a way. Hearing about Doug and their exciting dinner was difficult, but it was better than talking about Max. Besides, she was glad that her friend had had a good time.

But now Heather had to bring up Max. Frowning, Cindy examined Honor's saddle girth. The filly twisted her head in the crossties and lipped Cindy's jacket affectionately. Impulsively Cindy hugged Honor, her fingers sinking deep into the filly's glossy bay coat.

I really just want to hit the trails with my horse and

forget about Max, she thought. After a day of torturing herself over him, Cindy could barely stand to hear his name. But she knew she wouldn't be able to get Heather off the subject.

Heather tapped her foot on the concrete aisle. "Well?" she prodded. "So what is it with you and him?"

"Who knows? Nothing, I guess." Cindy expertly bridled Honor and adjusted the filly's black forelock around the headpiece.

"I *still* say Max likes you," Heather insisted. She dropped the flap on Chips's saddle and walked over to Cindy. Heather usually rode the trustworthy Appaloosa on the trails at Whitebrook.

"Why?" Cindy looked quickly at her best friend. Heather was usually very perceptive.

"It's obvious. I mean, before Max asked Laura to the skating party, he asked *you* everywhere," Heather pointed out.

"Big deal." Cindy shrugged. "You didn't see those red roses he gave Laura on Valentine's Day." Cindy groaned at the memory. She doubted if she could ever get that picture out of her mind. "I'm not going to go to the party at all. But you are, right?"

"Yeah, Doug asked me," Heather said shyly.

Cindy stared at her friend suspiciously. Heather blushed and looked away. "Heather, admit it," Cindy said. "You and Doug are a couple."

"Okay, okay." Heather held up her hands. "We did talk about it when we went to dinner. We decided that we're officially dating."

"And you didn't even tell me?" Cindy asked.

Heather's flush deepened. "Well, I didn't think you'd be interested. All you ever want to talk about is riding, Cindy."

Cindy slumped against Honor. *Heather's right*, she thought. *But what choice do I have, if I want to be good enough to ride in Dubai?* Honor looked around and nickered softly, as if she sympathized. Cindy reached up and absently rubbed her neck.

"So I guess that's why Max asked Laura to the party," Heather said. "He probably thought you didn't want to go."

"I wish everyone would stop telling me what I'm doing wrong," Cindy complained. She was tired of being attacked. Didn't anyone understand what she was trying to do? If she won in Dubai, then they'd have to understand.

"Cindy, I only want to help," Heather said firmly. "I still think Max is only taking Laura because he figured you were busy. So go to the party, and tell him how you feel."

"I couldn't!" Cindy gasped. "I already made a fool out of myself when I asked him to the party!"

"Do you want to stay home and just give up?" Heather said pointedly.

111

Cindy shook her head unhappily. She imagined herself sitting home, all by herself, while the rest of her class skated and had a great time. And she couldn't help feeling a gleam of hope at Heather's words. Maybe everything wasn't totally lost with Max. "I'll think about it," she said.

"You have to go to the party." Heather walked back to Chips and took a swipe at his neck with a finishing cloth.

"All right, all right, I'll go just to make you stop bothering me about it," Cindy snapped.

"Okay, good. I'll stop talking about it—but somebody's got to straighten you out," Heather told her.

Cindy drew a deep breath and tried to calm down. She knew her problems with Max weren't Heather's fault. "Sorry," she said as they led the horses out of the barn. "I didn't mean to snap at you."

"Don't worry about it." Heather shrugged. "I think I understand where you're coming from."

I don't really think anybody does, Cindy thought. *But before I go to that party, I'd better make sure I know what to say to Max or I'll just mess things up even more.*

"Is that you, Cindy?" Samantha asked later that afternoon as she opened the gate to the paddock.

"Yeah." Cindy tipped back her head to look at the

darkening sky. She sat on the ground, letting Honor graze around her feet. Cindy had said good-bye to Heather and then brought Honor out there.

Samantha walked over. She had a halter and lead rope slung over her shoulder. "Aren't you going to bring Honor up to the barn for dinner? I was just coming to get Fleet Street."

"In a minute." Cindy wasn't in a hurry to end her day with Honor. Besides, it was beautiful outside. Small, pink-edged clouds had caught the last light of the setting sun, and the grass felt cold and clean under her fingers. Cindy reached up to touch Honor's sleek shoulder. The filly quickly swung her head around and gratefully nudged Cindy's hand.

Samantha squatted down beside Cindy. "Did you have a good ride with Heather?" she asked.

"Yeah, it was okay." Cindy saw the two black fillies, Fleet Street and Lucky Chance, emerge out of the growing darkness. Fleet Street sniffed Samantha's shoulder.

"How's Heather doing?" Samantha tickled Fleet Street's nose.

"She's good," Cindy responded. "But I think she's a little annoyed with me. She said that the only thing I ever talk about is riding."

Samantha was quiet for a moment, looking at Cindy thoughtfully. "I can't say I disagree," she said finally.

Cindy fell back on her hands. "Are you mad at me, too?" she exclaimed. Then she felt a flash of anger. Samantha should understand how much dedication it took to be a jockey.

"No, I'm not mad. But I *am* worried," Samantha said bluntly. "You've become consumed by racing— and it's getting tiresome. You need to get your priorities straight and remember why you love riding in the first place."

"I already know why I love riding." What did Samantha know about Cindy's priorities?

"Then you'll prove it by what you do," Samantha continued. "The way you act now, I'd think that all you care about is winning your races, rather than the actual horses . . . or any of your relationships with people."

Cindy's cheeks burned. She couldn't believe that Samantha was questioning her devotion to the horses. "I'll just stop talking about racing to *you*, then," she said shortly.

"That's not my point. But you obviously don't want to hear what I'm saying." Samantha rose and clipped the lead rope to Fleet Street's halter. "You really should think about what I'm trying to tell you, though."

You really should leave me alone! Cindy thought, but she felt that if she opened her mouth, she'd start to cry. Silently she watched Samantha open the gate and lead out Fleet Street.

Honor touched Cindy's hands with her nose, as if she wondered what the fighting was about. Cindy burst into tears. "Everyone's ganging up on me and trying to distract me from the horses," she whispered. "Ashleigh, Max, Heather—and now Samantha's after me, too. Doesn't anyone understand, Honor?"

The beautiful filly blew out a sweet-smelling breath, as if to say that she would try to.

Cindy buried her face in Honor's thick, silky black mane. "Oh, Honor," she choked out. "Am I wrong about everything? I know I'm not! I know I have to work hard to win my races!"

Honor dropped her head back to the grass, slowly moving in the direction of the gate.

"I'd feel fine if I just won a race." Cindy wiped her eyes, trying to stop crying. "Why didn't I win when I tried so hard, Honor?"

The filly didn't seem to have the answer. She continued to peacefully crop the grass.

"I can't believe Sammy thinks I don't love the horses," Cindy muttered. "What a horrible thing to say. Where would she get that idea? Except..." Cindy thought back to her first race and the quick feeling of guilt she'd had afterward. She'd almost forgotten about Black Reason during the race. That had been partly because of her inexperience. But now Cindy realized she had been so worried about her ride, she had practically ignored her horse.

115

"Maybe Sammy wasn't trying to tell me not to work hard," Cindy murmured. "Maybe she was just saying I wasn't focusing on the right thing. I should work hard but focus on my horse and winning—not just on *me* and winning."

Honor tugged gently on the lead line. The five other fillies in the paddock had lined up at the gate, waiting to be taken up to the barn for dinner.

Cindy slowly got to her feet, brushing away a last tear. Samantha might have been right, but Cindy was still mad at her. "Sammy didn't have to be so mean," Cindy said to Honor. "She knows how stressed out I am." Cindy sighed unhappily. "Now I have to avoid her, too, just like Max. And it's going to be hard because Sammy's all over the place at home, just like Max is at school."

Honor pulled Cindy briskly toward the gate. She seemed to be saying that if Cindy couldn't make a decision, she'd make one for her.

"I lost Max, too, just like the race," Cindy mumbled. "I'm really having a losing streak." She paused for a moment, thinking about what she had just said. "Wait a minute. That's no joke. I really *did* lose Max the same way I lost the race. I acted like I didn't care about him, just like I did with Black Reason in the race. I didn't devote enough of myself to my relationship with Max or with Black Reason. I was only concentrating on winning." Cindy sighed. "And it's only now that I've lost Max that I realize what a mistake I made. How could I be so stupid?" Cindy groaned aloud.

Honor hauled Cindy the rest of the way to the gate, seeming to be out of patience with Cindy as well.

Samantha was walking back to the paddock from the barn. She was carrying several lead ropes. *I guess I owe Sammy an apology,* Cindy thought.

"Sammy, I'm sorry," she said as Samantha opened the gate. "I think you were right."

Samantha smiled and handed Cindy another lead rope. "It's okay. I just think you have the ability to be a fantastic jockey, Cindy. I don't want you to blow it."

"I won't." Cindy felt a surge of confidence. Since she knew why she had lost her first race, she was sure she'd win the next one.

Now I just have to get up the nerve to talk to Max, Cindy said to herself as she clipped a lead line to Calamity Jane's halter to take the two fillies up to the barn together. Cindy imagined herself stammering and saying all the wrong things as she tried to apologize to Max. She felt embarrassed just thinking about it. *Apologizing to him won't be much easier than winning a race!*

9

"CINDY, WHERE HAVE YOU BEEN?" HEATHER CALLED, GLID-
ing across the ice at the skating rink that Saturday.
"The party started an hour ago!"

"I was calling the track about Champion." Cindy
stood nervously at the edge of the large rink in her
skates, watching her classmates on the ice. The
tenth-grade social planning committee had reserved
the entire rink for the evening, so they had plenty of
room.

Some of the kids were good skaters and sailed
across the ice gracefully, while others shuffled along,
clinging to the rail as they struggled to balance themselves. Yet everyone seemed to be having a great

time. But when Cindy scanned the rink, she didn't see Max anywhere.

Heather wobbled to a stop in front of her. She was wearing a bright blue sweater that complemented her light blond hair. "Why did you call the track now?" she asked. "You know Champion's always fine."

"Yeah, but I miss him. I wanted to find out if he missed me, too." Cindy shrugged. "And I was trying to get up my nerve to come here," she admitted sheepishly.

Heather held on to the rail and lifted her foot to clean the ice off her blade. "Well, I'm glad that you finally came."

"Is Max here?" Cindy whispered nervously.

"Yeah, he's over at the snack bar," Heather told her.

Cindy looked around to make sure no one was listening. "Look, Heather, maybe my coming wasn't such a good idea. I mean, I haven't talked to Max all week." Cindy thought she knew what she should say to him, but she just hadn't had the guts to approach him. She'd avoided him all week at school after that disastrous Valentine's Day, and the silence grew between them. By Thursday, Max had given up trying to talk to her. She still saw him looking at her sometimes in class and in the hallways, but Cindy doubted that meant much.

Doug skated up to them. "How's it going, Cindy?" he said.

"Okay." Cindy forced a smile. With his curly blond hair and blue eyes, Doug was a perfect skating partner for Heather. They made an adorable couple. "How are you, Doug?"

"Pretty good," he said, smiling at Heather and reaching for her hand. "C'mon, let's skate."

Heather looked questioningly at Cindy.

"Go ahead," Cindy said brightly. "I'll be right behind you."

"Okay, but come get me if you need me." Heather put her mittened hand in Doug's.

"Don't worry about it," Cindy assured her. *What could be more fun than this?* Cindy thought miserably as she skated after Heather and Doug. They were still holding hands, making it clear to everyone that they were a couple.

Cindy glanced back and almost tripped over her skates. Max was just stepping onto the ice.

He looks so cute. Cindy's heart beat faster as she looked at Max's thick dark hair and tall, athletic build. Seemingly effortlessly, he skated across the ice at top speed.

Cindy sighed. It seemed impossible now that she'd ever had somebody as cool as him as her boyfriend. She didn't deserve him.

Heather dropped back to skate with Cindy. "There's Max!" she hissed, giving Cindy a little push. "Talk to him now."

Cindy almost lost her balance. She skated over to the side of the rink and gripped the rail, shaking her head. "Are you kidding? The whole rink is watching!"

"Suit yourself," Heather told her. "But this whole situation is just going to get worse." Heather skated back to Doug at the center of the ice.

Maybe if Max sees me, he'll come over and talk to me, Cindy hoped. She glided smoothly across the ice, circling the rink. She knew she was a good skater. At the far side of the rink Cindy slid to a graceful stop, crisply sinking both blades sideways into the ice. Then she looked back to see if Max was watching.

Her heart sank as she saw that Max was at the center of a group playing crack the whip. Melissa and Sharon held his hands, and Doug and Heather had linked onto the end of the chain. Cindy thought she saw Laura, but at that moment the chain of people broke up into a pile, laughing and falling, and she couldn't be sure.

Cindy took a deep breath. *Okay, I guess I have to swallow my pride and go talk to him now,* she thought, skating toward the human chain.

Before she could get there, the rink guards broke up the game. Cindy spotted Laura, getting up from the ice next to Max. She was wearing a short red skating skirt with black tights and a black sweater.

"Cindy, when did you show up?" Laura called to her.

"Yeah, we were looking for you," Max added.

I'll just bet, Cindy thought. Before she could speak, Laura grabbed Max's hand and skated off with him.

"Oh, Cindy—I'm sorry," Heather said softly.

"Me too." Cindy realized that she was standing alone in the middle of the rink, looking like a total fool. "I'm going home," she whispered hoarsely. Cindy skated rapidly toward the opening in the rink, unsucessfully fighting back the tears.

I'll just call Sammy to come get me, she thought. Stifling a sob, Cindy pulled off her mittens to wipe away her tears. She stepped blindly off the ice.

A cold shower of fine snow blew over her as someone stopped sharply behind her. Cindy turned slowly, shaking the snow off her cold hands. She found herself staring straight at Max. His cheeks were flushed from skating, and his dark hair was tousled.

"Why are you going in?" he asked. "Are you cold?"

"No!" Cindy said angrily. How could Max pretend nothing was wrong when she was suffering like this? Cindy turned around and walked as quickly as she could to the snack bar. After a few strides she stubbed her toepick on the rubber matting and almost fell into the snack machines.

Max stomped after her. "What is with you lately?" he shouted. "You wouldn't talk to me all week, and now you're running away again. What's the matter—are you going to a horse race or something?"

Furious, Cindy whirled to face him. She saw several of their classmates watching them with interest, but she didn't care. If Max wanted to shout at her in front of everyone, that was just fine with her. "I'm not going anywhere!" she cried. "But what have you been doing?"

"What are you talking about?" The expression on Max's handsome face was a complete mix of confusion, anger, and impatience.

"Give me a break." Cindy rolled her eyes.

"I really *don't* know what you're talking about, Cindy." Max sounded exasperated. "Would you please clue me in on why you're so mad at me?"

"Did you think I *liked* it when you gave Laura roses on Valentine's Day?" Cindy shot back. Tears filled Cindy's eyes again. She clomped over to a bench and sat down to take off her skates.

"Those roses were for you." Max sat beside her.

Cindy stared at him. "For me? But—"

"I bought them for you," Max said. "But you ran away from me. I felt like an idiot carrying them around, so I finally gave them to Laura. And I only asked Laura to the skating party because I thought you were too busy to come."

So that's what happened, Cindy thought, weak with relief. *I can't believe I worried myself sick for almost a week over nothing.*

"Are you satisfied now?" Max sounded angry.

"Not quite." Cindy felt a lot better, but she still had to know something. She paused for a moment to collect her thoughts. Then she looked straight into his eyes and asked, "Do you want to be my boyfriend or not?"

"I did want to, but . . ." Max began, his voice trailing off.

Cindy dropped her gaze and squeezed her trembling hands. *So that's his answer. I've been rejected!*

"Look at me, would you?" Max asked.

Cindy forced herself to lift her eyes. Max was staring at her quizzically. He was very close to her, almost close enough to kiss her. . . .

He leaned forward, and his lips brushed hers in a quick kiss.

Cindy closed her eyes, blissfully savoring the feel of Max's lips on hers and the strong grip of his hands on her shoulders. She realized just how much she'd missed their very special closeness.

Max sat back. "Look, Cindy, you never have any time for me. How can we be a couple if we don't see each other? Maybe we should just be friends."

Cindy shook her head. She was sure that she didn't want to lose Max now. "I'll make more time for us," she promised.

"Will you?" Max searched her face, as if he were trying to read her thoughts.

"Yes. But Max . . ." Cindy hesitated. "I *am* going to be really busy for a while. I'm leaving Monday for Gulfstream, and I won't be back until after the Dubai World Cup. That means in just two days I'm leaving Whitebrook for more than a month."

"We could do something tomorrow," Max pointed out.

Cindy drew a deep breath. She didn't want Max to be angry again, but she had to tell him the truth. "I'm riding tomorrow. I have to work really hard since I'm competing on Champion against Ashleigh. Did you even know we're both riding in Dubai?"

"Of course—Heather told me." Max looked at her intently. "Did you really think I didn't care what you were doing all this time?"

"Well, I thought you might be sick of hearing about the horses," Cindy admitted.

"You know that I love horses," Max said. "And I think it's incredible that you're going to Dubai. It's just when you went on and on about horses and racing, you acted like you could be talking to anybody. I didn't think you cared about *me*."

"Well, I do." Cindy looked at him timidly. "So, how do you feel about Laura?"

"That she's not you. Laura and I are just friends— we talked about it. She knows that I like you." Max kissed Cindy's forehead. "Look, you have to eat, even if you're in training. How about I take you out to dinner tomorrow? It'll be our first date as an official couple."

"I can't wait." Cindy jumped to her feet and held out her hands. "Come on!" Suddenly she felt like skating all night.

10

ON SUNDAY EVENING CINDY DROPPED THE RACING MAGA-zine she had been reading on her bed and stepped over to the mirror to study her reflection. In just a few minutes Max would arrive for their date. It was also the last time they would see each other before Cindy's trip to Dubai. Cindy wanted to look her best, so that the last time she saw Max would be as perfect as possible.

"Cindy, Max is here," Samantha called up the stairs.

"I'll be there in a second." Cindy gazed critically at the mirror. She and Heather had decided that a simple, elegant look was Cindy's style. Heather had helped Cindy pick out a brown suede skirt, a black V-neck sweater and low black ankle boots. Cindy had French-braided her hair and applied just a touch of lip gloss and eye makeup.

"I'm old enough to ride in the Dubai World Cup," she murmured. "Maybe I can finally handle an official date with Max."

Max looked around the doorway. "You look great," he said, smiling.

Cindy's hand flew to her cheek. "Max—you scared me!" Cindy was taken aback at how cute Max looked in his khaki pants and burgundy sweater.

She flushed, suddenly feeling shy. "You look good, too," she managed to say.

"Let's go." Max held out his hand. "I made reservations at Chez François—it's one of the best French restaurants in Lexington. You said you liked French food, right?"

Cindy nodded. She did like French food—she'd had it at several tracks around the country. She smiled. It was sweet of Max to remember that.

The living room was empty. "Thank goodness Beth is teaching an evening aerobics class," Cindy said. "She's not here to ambush us with her camera."

"But *I* am." Samantha walked out of the kitchen, holding Kevin with one hand and a camera with the other.

"Sammy!" Cindy groaned. "Traitor!"

"One picture for posterity." Samantha set down Kevin and aimed the camera.

Kevin ran over to Cindy. "Oh, you want to be in the picture?" Cindy gathered the little boy close, and Kevin snuggled in her arms. Cindy smiled down at him. She wouldn't see much of her little brother for a while. Beth and Kevin were only going to come to Gulfstream once before Dubai, and they wouldn't be going to the United Arab Emirates at all.

The flash went off. "Very nice." Samantha put the camera down. "Okay, now you can go. Have fun."

"So much for a dignified exit," Cindy complained to Max as they walked down the path to his car. But she had to admit that Kevin and Samantha had broken the ice. Cindy wasn't nearly as nervous as she had been at first.

Max opened the car door for her. "You're lucky to have a brother and sister," he said. "With just my mom and me, I get lonely sometimes. And my mom's out on call a lot."

"I think I'm lucky, too—most of the time." Cindy glanced around the car. "Hey, is this new?"

"Yes, it is." Max smiled broadly as he pulled out of the driveway. "You noticed I got a car!"

"Of course I noticed," Cindy responded. "Do you think I only notice something new if it has four legs?"

"Yes," Max said with a laugh.

Cindy punched him playfully. "That's not true!"

129

Max punched her back and they exchanged a brief smile before Max turned his eyes to the road.

Max parked the car in the crowded restaurant parking lot and offered Cindy his arm. "This should be good," he said. "I had to call two weeks ahead to get reservations."

Cindy stopped dead. "How did you know we'd be coming here? We weren't even on speaking terms last week!"

Max squeezed her arm. "I took a chance. That's one of the things I was trying to talk to you about at school."

"That's so sweet. Thanks for not canceling the reservation while we were arguing." Cindy couldn't believe how thoughtful Max was.

"I guess I never lost hope." Max stopped Cindy just before the door to the restaurant and kissed her gently.

"I'm glad you didn't," she whispered.

Cindy hesitated in the doorway to the restaurant, stunned by the glittering chandeliers, the huge, panoramic windows, and the elegant, well-dressed diners quietly conversing at the tables.

The maitre d' showed them to a window table with a sweeping view of the lights of Lexington. "It's so beautiful," Cindy said quietly.

"Just like you." Max reached for her hand.

Cindy smiled, flattered by Max's compliment. This

date was going better than she had imagined. She and Max were still good friends, but now there was even more of a bond between them.

The waiter read the list of dinner specials while Cindy glanced at the menu. She saw several entrées that she'd had at other restaurants. "I'll try the red snapper special," she ordered.

"And I'll have the crab soufflé." Max closed his menu.

The waiter walked away, and Cindy tried to think of what to talk about. She didn't want Max to think she was boring. *I'm not going to bring up horses at all*, she thought determinedly. *I'll have plenty of time to talk about horses—and to them—when I'm back at Gulfstream.*

Max set down his piece of bread. "So tell me about your next race," he said. "You're going to ride against Ashleigh?"

"Yes. But we don't have to talk about that," Cindy said politely.

Max groaned. "Cindy! I told you, I don't mind talking about horses as long as I feel that you care about me, too. What do you want to talk about?"

"Um . . . shopping?" Cindy teased.

Max laughed. "Any other suggestions?"

Cindy propped her head in her hands. "You know, I haven't really been able to talk to anybody about riding against Ashleigh. In some ways I'm looking forward to it. But I'm kind of dreading it, too."

Max nodded. "She's really been your teacher since you came to Whitebrook."

"Yeah, the most important one. Ashleigh taught me almost everything I know about riding. And I've always looked up to her so much. I still do—I mean, she's a fantastic rider. It's going to be tough to race against her." Cindy glanced out the window at the twinkling lights of Lexington. In just over a month she'd be in Dubai in the United Arab Emirates, gazing at the lights of a city half a world away.

I wonder how it will all end? she thought. *If I do well at Gulfstream and make it as Champion's jockey, will we win at Dubai or lose to Ashleigh and Limitless?*

"I guess you'll find out soon enough what it'll be like to ride against Ashleigh," Max said, seeming to read her thoughts.

"Well, I've got one more race with Black Reason before I go up against Ashleigh," Cindy said. "If I don't do well in that, then I don't have anything to worry about."

"You're smart and talented and you're going to win your next race," Max said firmly. "I know it."

"Thanks." Cindy looked at Max intently. "It means so much to me to hear you say that. You know, maybe a little bit of the reason I lost my first race was that you and I weren't getting along. I couldn't seem to concentrate very well."

"But we're okay now. So get out on the track and knock 'em dead," Max instructed, smiling.

The waiter stepped up to the table to serve their dinners. "For mademoiselle," he said, deftly placing Cindy's entrée in front of her.

Cindy picked up her fork and took a bite of the red snapper. It was hot, delicately cooked and seasoned, and absolutely delicious. She offered Max some.

"Mmm, that's really good," he said, returning her fork. He paused and then added, "I was just thinking how lucky you are to ride at the level you do. Even riding in an allowance race on Black Reason is pretty amazing at our age."

"I know—I can still hardly believe that all of this is happening to me. But not *everything* about riding in races is good—I have to go away for so long." Cindy wiped her mouth with her napkin. "Just when we got things worked out, I have to leave. Are you really okay with that?"

Max shrugged. "I won't say it makes me happy, but I know how important racing is to you. So it's okay with me, on one condition."

"What's that?" Cindy looked across the table at him. From the warm look on Max's face, she thought she would like his condition.

"Will you think about me when you're in Dubai?" he asked.

"Of course—every day," Cindy promised. "I just wish you could come with me." Half closing her eyes, Cindy imagined herself and Max roaming hand in hand through the shifting, whispering dunes of the Arabian desert. *That would be so cool,* she thought with a sigh.

The waiter returned. "Would mademoiselle care for dessert this evening? Tonight we have a rich chocolate mousse or an eclair with fresh whipped cream."

Cindy snapped out of her reverie. She looked questioningly at Max. "How can I choose?" she asked. "They're both my favorites."

"We'll take one of each," Max said. "With two forks."

"That's my boyfriend." Cindy grinned.

"I think I know you pretty well." Max grinned back.

After they had devoured the rich desserts and sipped their cappuccinos, Max glanced at his watch. "Wow, it's after eleven. We'd better get you back. I know you have to get up early."

"Yeah, I do." Cindy reluctantly pushed back her chair. She'd had such a good time, she didn't want the evening to end.

During the car ride home Cindy rested her head lightly on Max's shoulder. It felt natural and comfortable.

At the doorway to the McLeans' cottage Max took Cindy's hands in his and gently squeezed them. "I'm going to miss you," he said. "I'll think about you every second you're riding in your races."

"It'll be almost like you're there." Cindy put her arms around Max's neck. His dark hair gleamed in the bright light of the moon, slowly sinking on the horizon. Suddenly Cindy never wanted to let him go.

Max bent his head to hers. As Cindy's lips met his in a passionate kiss she felt transported to another world, as far away and unknown as Arabia. Cindy's thoughts spun dizzily as she and Max kissed again.

At last Cindy drew back. "Wow," she said softly. "That was pretty amazing."

"Yeah," Max agreed. "It was."

Cindy searched his face, wishing she could memorize it. In many ways it was the same face she'd known since she was eleven years old. But now his eyes expressed how much he cared for her. *That's been there for a while,* Cindy realized. *I just didn't notice.*

"I'd better go," Max whispered. "Good luck, Cindy. I promise I'll see you ride in a race someday."

Cindy nodded, unable to speak. Max kissed her quickly on her cheek, then walked down the path to his car.

Cindy dropped down on the stoop and watched him drive away. Max's loving support had made her feel strong and confident. But she already felt lonely without him.

"It's just going to get worse," she murmured. "I'll be all alone on the track. Even Ashleigh won't be on my side."

135

One of the stallions whinnied loudly from the barn, the sound echoing through the quiet night. Cindy thought she recognized Glory's voice. She smiled a little.

"Well, I won't be quite alone out there," Cindy said softly as she stood up to go inside. "Black Reason and Champion will be with me."

11

"ARE YOU READY?" IAN ASKED CINDY FIVE DAYS LATER AS HE and Samantha led Black Reason over to her from the walking ring. The call had just come for riders up in Cindy's second race at Gulfstream, a seven-furlong allowance race. Cindy, dressed in her sky blue and white jockey's silks, was waiting with Ashleigh at the side of the walking ring.

Cindy nodded, her pulse quickening. *This time I really am ready*, she thought. *I've got my head straight, and I know exactly what I'm doing.*

Black Reason tossed his head, shaking his silky black mane, and pawed the ground. He seemed just as eager as Cindy to take on the competition.

"He looks good," Ashleigh said.

"He ought to," Cindy replied quickly. "I've taken him and Champion out every day since I got here." Both colts had gone very well for her, and Cindy had felt her confidence growing with each ride.

"Let me give you a leg up, Cindy." Ian cupped his hands, and Cindy sprang lightly into the tiny racing saddle. Gathering her reins, she glanced around. This time it didn't seem so disorienting to be high above the heads of the crowd.

"I'm glad you drew a position near the rail," Samantha said, looking up at her.

"Yeah, that's better than in my first race," Cindy answered.

"The competition's tougher this time," Ashleigh warned. "Two stakes horses are running. First Call is coming off an injury, but he won impressively in the seven-furlong Sport Page Handicap at Aqueduct in the fall. Winner's Three recently won the Clark Stakes at a mile and eighth—"

"I know. He'll have something left at the end," Cindy interrupted. She had read up on all the horses in the field. Personally Cindy was more worried about Right of Passage, a black colt who had won his last sprint at Gulfstream by six lengths. He was definitely at the top of his game.

Cindy couldn't help frowning at Ashleigh. Why was she being so negative? "Those horses are tough, but

Black Reason's last workout was the fastest of any horse in the field," Cindy reminded Ashleigh. Several of the other jockeys on the track had congratulated Cindy.

"I'm not trying to scare you," Ashleigh said quickly. "I just want you to be prepared."

"Try to get Black Reason away quickly at the break." Ian looked up at her.

"I will. You already told me that, Dad." Black Reason was chomping on the bit and bowing his head against her restraint. Cindy patted the colt's black shoulder, trying to distract him. She wished everyone would quit giving her advice and let her ride her race.

"Here comes your exercise pony, Cindy," Mike said. "Hi, Jake," he added to the rider. Jake Salinas, a man in his fifties, was a former jockey. He was riding a heavyset chestnut quarter horse gelding, who would accompany Black Reason to the track.

Cindy knew that Ashleigh, Mike, and Ian had decided to have Black Reason ponied for this race. Most racehorses used an exercise pony to keep them calm until they were loaded in the gate. Champion wouldn't tolerate one, but Black Reason seemed to like the company.

"Here we go," said Jake, taking hold of Black Reason's reins.

"Good luck, Cindy!" Beth waved from group of onlookers at the edge of the walking ring.

"Thanks!" Cindy felt a surge of pride and excitement as she left the Whitebrook group and headed for the tunnel to the track with just the exercise pony. She knew what to expect out on the track this time, and she felt sure that she'd know exactly what to do.

"Black Reason's a good horse," Jake said encouragingly as they trotted toward the starting gate, positioned on the far side of the track. "I think you've got a real shot at winning."

"Me too!" Cindy posted rapidly to the trot in her short stirrups. *I've got to be as good as my colt is*, she thought. *But today I'm going to be!*

Black Reason loaded in the two position of the gate, in the stall between First Call and Right Passage. The back gate of the stall clanged loudly behind them. Cindy leaned forward, concentrating completely on what she had to do—break Black Reason fast out of the gate.

"Almost time, boy," she murmured as the seven other horses loaded into the gate with thumps and bumps.

Black Reason lifted lightly on his hind legs, staring out through the bars at the track. "Steady," Cindy soothed. "I want you on your toes, not climbing the walls."

The colt seemed to understand. He trembled with nervous energy, but his front hooves stayed on the ground.

Cindy crouched over his neck. *Get ready*, she told herself. *Only a couple of seconds more. Stay on top of it. . . .*

The gates crashed open. "And they're off!" the announcer called. "It's Black Reason getting off first. Winner's Three is right there; back one to First Call. . . ."

Cindy felt a quick rush of joy. "We're out in front!" she whispered. "I did it!"

The next instant the field rushed up around them. Winner's Three, First Call, and Right of Passage pounded at Black Reason's flanks and heels. First Call's jockey was trying to squeeze his colt through a small hole on the inside.

They're all trying to pass us, just like in my first race. But I won't let them, Cindy told herself fiercely. *Not this time!*

"Hang on to the lead, boy," she called, letting out the reins a notch. "Just a little faster!"

The colt responded with a leap of speed. But the other three colts stayed right up with them. "More, Reason!" Cindy cried, flattening her position over Black Reason's neck. She knew that by asking the colt for so much early speed she risked burning him out, but they just had to stay ahead of the field!

Black Reason surged ahead, running strongly about half a length ahead of the other front-runners.

"Yes!" Cindy cried. "Thanks, boy!" The colt leaned into the far turn, hugging the rail, and blazed into the stretch. With a powerful flick of his legs Black Reason changed leads and slowly drew away from the rest of the field. Glancing quickly over her shoulder, Cindy saw that they'd increased their lead from half a length to nearly two lengths over Winner's Three! "Not much farther, Reason," she called. "We're going to win it!"

"Black Reason is still on the lead by two," she heard the announcer call. "But wait! Here come First Call and Winner's Three to challenge! They're not out of this race. And Right of Passage is driving like a machine on the outside!"

Cindy didn't have to look to know just how quickly the three closers were eating into Black Reason's lead. They were coming up at what seemed like supersonic speed! The thunder of the other colts' hooves drummed into Cindy's ears as Right of Passage's nose drew even with Black Reason's flank.

But Cindy was sure she knew just how much horse she had left. It was time to make her move!

"Now, Reason," she cried, kneading her hands into the colt's neck. "Go for it—let's put them away!"

Black Reason dug valiantly into the soft dirt of the track, his powerful shoulder muscles bulging as he took huge strides toward the finish. But the closers were less than a length behind and still gaining!

This is going to be so close. Cindy prayed she'd been right about how much strength Black Reason had left. She might have used him up at the beginning of the race. But she had faith in her colt. She knew he wanted to win as much as she did!

"Give it all you've got, boy," she cried.

Black Reason responded with a final surge of speed. Cindy thought the hoofbeats behind were gaining more slowly, but she didn't dare look back. *Just one more furlong*, she thought, gritting her teeth.

Cindy heard the quick, sharp snorts of Right of Passage as the other black colt pulled nearly even with Black Reason. The horses were burning up the track at nearly forty miles an hour, just inches apart. But they seemed almost to be standing still as Right of Passage slowly cut into Black Reason's lead.

Black Reason's neck, shoulders, and flanks glittered with sweat, and his breaths came in quick, loud snorts. Cindy knew he didn't have any more speed to give. If only he could hang on!

Black Reason wasn't slowing. His hoofbeats tireless and steady, the colt pounded for the wire. *Just a few more strides*, Cindy thought, gripping Black Reason's mane tightly. *Four more . . . three . . .* Right of Passage was still inching up on Black Reason, but there was the wire!

"The Whitebrook colt comes through!" the announcer called. "Black Reason wins it by a nose!"

Laughing with sheer delight, Cindy stood in her stirrups and patted the colt's wet neck. "That's the way, boy!" she said breathlessly. "You were wonderful!"

Tired as he was, the black colt flicked back an ear to acknowledge her familiar voice. Cindy pulled him down to a trot, then circled him to return to the gap— and the winner's circle!

"Way to go, Cindy," Samantha yelled as Cindy rode up to her.

"Nice one!" Mike called.

Cindy saw that her whole family, plus everybody else from Whitebrook who was at Gulfstream, had gathered by the gap to congratulate her. In a daze Cindy slipped out of the saddle and tried to stand on her weak knees. Mark grabbed her elbow to steady her, then took Black Reason's reins. "I did it!" Cindy cried. "I won a race!"

"You sure did." Ian smiled broadly. "I'm so proud of you, honey."

"Excellent, Cindy," Mark said, giving her a high five.

Cindy quickly unfastened Black Reason's saddle and weighed out at the scale. Her family and friends were already waiting in the winner's circle with Black Reason and the press. *This time I won't be standing off to the side of the pictures!* Cindy thought blissfully. "I can't believe how fantastic it feels to stand here as a winning jockey!" she whispered to Ashleigh.

"It's the best." Ashleigh's gaze was warm.

"What did you think of my race?" Cindy asked. Cindy knew she'd ridden well, but would Ashleigh think she'd earned her way to Dubai as Champion's jockey?

Ashleigh's face told her all she needed to know. "You'll be going to Dubai," she said, grinning broadly. "Black Reason ran his race only a tick slower than the track record!"

Joyfully Cindy hugged Black Reason. "Dubai, here I come! Wow, I can't believe we went that fast. I wasn't even thinking about it!"

"It's true," Samantha confirmed. "Your first win, and you're already practically in the record books."

"Thanks, Cindy," Mike said. "A win like that is good PR for Whitebrook."

Cindy shook her head, almost overcome by the good news. She had waited so long to succeed as a jockey, she could hardly believe her dream had come true.

Black Reason stood very close to Cindy, still huffing out quick breaths, as the cameras clicked. Cindy pressed her cheek against his damp mane. "Thank *you*, boy," she whispered. "I know you put in an incredible effort."

The colt gently nuzzled her hand. He seemed to be saying that no thanks were needed between such good friends.

"Let's get Reason back to the barn," Mark urged. "He's pretty tired."

"Right," Cindy agreed.

"We'll take over here," Ian said. "See you back at the barn, sweetie."

With Mark's help, Cindy pushed a path through the crowd and led Black Reason toward the backside.

"Made it," Mark commented as they broke free of the onlookers.

"Not that many people were at the winner's circle—I mean, this was just an allowance race." Cindy shrugged. "But the crowd's going to be huge in Dubai!"

"So you're really going as Champion's jockey, huh?" Mark said.

"That's what Ashleigh said." Cindy watched Black Reason walk, expertly checking for signs of soreness. He seemed tired but okay.

"Well, good luck," Mark said. "You'll need it, racing against Ashleigh."

"I guess I will." Cindy felt a nervous fluttering in her stomach when she thought about racing against Ashleigh—Cindy looked up to her so much. But she was also annoyed that after the ride she'd just put in, Mark still seemed to doubt her abilities. "But I think that I just showed that I'm a pretty good jockey myself," she said, shooting Mark an irritated glance.

"Well, yeah. And you do have the better horse," Mark replied. "A Triple Crown champion comes around only once in most jockeys' careers."

"That's not why—" Cindy began as they reached the shed row.

"Back in a sec," Mark said. "I'll catch up with you."

Cindy began walking Black Reason around the stable yard. She was upset by Mark's comments. *I guess he still thinks I'm a second-rate jockey*, she thought. *I need a stakes victory before anyone will take me seriously. Well, just wait till Dubai!*

Mark rejoined Cindy and Black Reason, and they made a couple of circuits around the quiet stable yard. Black Reason's breathing was soon back to normal. He seemed relaxed and happy as he followed Cindy closely.

"I think he came out of the race fine," Mark said.

"So do I." Cindy was still bothered by Mark's attitude about her race. She wanted to prove to him that she knew what she was doing, even if she hadn't won the biggest races yet. "You know what? I really understand now how to be a top jockey."

"You do?" Mark raised a quizzical eyebrow.

"Yes," Cindy said firmly. "It's when a jockey channels concentration, work, and experience into her ride, so that she goes for the win with all her heart."

Mark looked at her admiringly. "That sounds about right."

"And then she wins!" Cindy thrust a triumphant fist into the air. Black Reason spooked, startled by the abrupt movement and her loud voice.

"Hey, don't get carried away." Mark laughed.

"I won't." Cindy rubbed Black Reason's ear. After a few seconds the colt tipped it toward her. He was over his fright. "Nothing can stop me now," Cindy said confidently. "I'm on my way to Dubai."

12

"WHICH OF THE HORSES DO YOU WANT ME TO EXERCISE today?" Cindy asked Ashleigh a week later, walking down the shed row toward the older jockey. Ashleigh was brushing Limitless Time in front of his stall.

Champion hung his head over the netting of his stall, and Cindy stopped to pet his nose. Champion rubbed the side of his head against her arm contentedly.

"He seems like a different horse these days," Vic commented as he passed with a wheelbarrow. "He's quit acting up."

"Ashleigh said he was bored." Cindy could see how Champion got that way. She looked impatiently up the shed row at Ashleigh, who hadn't yet given her an answer about which horse to take out. Cindy wished she could just read the horses' exercise charts in the tack room and get going. But Ashleigh always wanted the exercise riders to check with her first.

Ashleigh tossed Limitless's brushes into his trunk. "Sorry to keep you waiting, Cindy," she said. "I was trying to plan out a complicated day. Why don't you ride Champion first? I bet he'd like that."

"Great!" Cindy was already heading for the tack room to get Champion's saddle and bridle.

"I'll meet you on the track," Ashleigh said. "I want to put Limitless through his paces."

"Okay." Cindy dropped Champion's tack on the trunk in front of his stall. "Let's hurry up and get you brushed, boy—we're going for a ride!" She quickly led the colt out of his stall and tied him.

Cindy had exercised Champion twice since she'd returned to Gulfstream over a week ago. Ashleigh had ridden him on the days Cindy hadn't, saying something about a "transition phase." Cindy hoped that Ashleigh wanted to move on today and let Cindy be Champion's sole rider.

Champion craned his neck around as Cindy brushed him, watching her every move. "I'm not going away again for a long time," she reassured the colt, brushing his glossy dark brown shoulder. "Don't worry. We have lots to do first."

Suddenly Champion seized the brush with his teeth

and yanked. "Oh, no, you don't." Cindy pulled hard on the brush and managed to win the tug-of-war.

Champion looked so disappointed that his trick hadn't worked, Cindy dropped the brush and hugged him. "You want attention, don't you?" she asked. When she'd first come back to Gulfstream, Champion had been so thrilled to see her, he'd almost climbed out of his stall. Cindy finally had to go inside with him to calm him down.

Cindy ran her hands through Champion's thick, almost black mane and closed her eyes for a second. It felt wonderful to be back with her horse. Cindy had driven herself so hard at home, working on her riding, she hadn't really let herself think about how much she missed him.

Champion was still for a few moments, sniffing her hair. Then he wriggled impatiently in her arms. He seemed to be asking if they could hurry up and get going.

"You really are bold, do you know that?" Cindy asked with a laugh. "Okay, I won't hold you up any longer."

She finished brushing Champion until his coat shone, combed his long mane and tail, and tacked him up. The colt eagerly marched after her into the stable yard, affectionately pushing her along with his nose.

"Let's put in a really good workout today,

Champion," Cindy said as she gathered the colt's reins and climbed on the mounting block. "You know we're really still on trial about Dubai. If I make one mistake, I won't be riding you there."

The early morning was cool and damp, fresh from the rain of the night before, as Cindy walked Champion to the track. The air smelled sweetly of oranges, and the colt's way of going was easy and sure. Cindy shook back her hair, feeling blissfully happy and privileged. *Nothing beats being a jockey!* she thought.

"Ashleigh wants you to work Champion half a mile today," Mike called from the trainer's tower. With Ashleigh, he and Ian were supervising Champion, Limitless, and the other Whitebrook horses at Gulfstream.

"Got it," Cindy called back.

"Warm Champion up well, then come back and we'll talk before you work him," Ian said.

Cindy waved to show that she understood. The track was crowded, with dozens of horses moving on and off it as they began or finished their morning exercise. Cindy felt a surge of excitement at the thought of being part of the bustle. "This is the big time, boy," she said softly to Champion. "It's a lot different from Whitebrook."

The colt flicked back his small, finely shaped ears in acknowledgment. Cindy was glad that he seemed to be handling the confusion on the track well. Champion was turning his head a little, watching the other horses, but he seemed focused on their ride.

Cindy cued Champion for a walk, moving him near the outside rail. After a furlong she asked him for a trot. Champion floated around the track, his prominent eyes bright. "Now let's gallop," Cindy murmured, rising over the colt's neck. "Easy does it, though, until you're warmed up." Cindy checked Champion slightly to let a small gray filly pass on the inside, then guided him closer to the rail. "Okay!"

Champion plunged into a gallop at Cindy's signal, his strides even and purposeful. Cindy kept her mind on her job, but she couldn't help smiling broadly as the marker posts whipped by. Even at a warm-up gallop Champion was still airborne for an incredible length of time with every stride. He was almost flying over the track. Even if Champion hadn't won the Triple Crown, Cindy would have known she was riding a miracle horse.

Keeping a careful eye out for traffic, she circled the track once. She glimpsed Ashleigh and Limitless warming up on the clubhouse turn.

"Stay here for a few seconds," Ian said when Cindy drew Champion up at the gap. "Good going, sweetheart."

Cindy grinned with excitement and satisfaction. "What's next?" she asked. "Why are we waiting?"

"We're going to work Champion with Limitless," Mike replied.

"Oh," Cindy said slowly. She supposed she should have known that the two colts might go out against each other. *I'm not really competing against Ashleigh right now,* she thought. *It's just exercise.* But Cindy's heart began to pound.

Her head jerked around at the heavy staccato sound of hooves on the track. Ashleigh was galloping Limitless Time into the stretch.

Ashleigh was crouched over Limitless's neck, her hands tight on the black colt's neck, her cheek almost resting against his mane. Limitless switched leads in one fluid motion, Ashleigh's cue to him too subtle for Cindy to see. The colt moved in a perfectly straight line for the wire. Cindy knew that the other jockey didn't see her—Ashleigh was much too focused on her ride.

"Nice, Ash," Mike called as Ashleigh began pulling Limitless up. Ashleigh touched her crop to her helmet in salute.

Cindy wiped her sweating hands on her jeans. *How can I ride against Ashleigh?* she thought. *Am I anywhere near that good?*

"The track's a little slippery," Ashleigh said as she rode up to the gap. Cindy noticed that Ashleigh had a serious expression. She wasn't beaming and excited because she'd just put in a fantastic ride on a stakes horse. Cindy reminded herself to calm down and act a little more professional.

"Be careful out there, Cindy," Ian said with a worried look. "Don't slip and fall."

"We won't." Cindy tried not to sound irritated. Neither her dad nor Mike was telling Ashleigh to be careful.

Ashleigh patted Limitless's gleaming black neck. "Let's go, Cindy," she said. "This is our time slot." Cindy knew Ashleigh must have notified the official clocker that they were working the horses now.

Without waiting for a reply, Ashleigh trotted off on Limitless. Cindy instantly cued Champion to follow. She wasn't going to be left in anybody's dust—or mud.

"If I just pay attention to what I'm doing and don't worry about Ashleigh, I'll be fine," Cindy muttered as she trotted Champion after Limitless. Cindy felt a quick rush of confidence as she remembered how well Champion had gone for her in his gallop just minutes before. "I won my last race after an incredible ride, and Champion is an even better horse than Black Reason," she reminded herself. "We won't lose here."

Ashleigh put Limitless into a slow gallop. Cindy followed suit, asking Champion for a bit more until the two colts were galloping neck and neck. Ashleigh gradually guided Limitless toward the inside until he was right next to the rail, in the lane for high speed.

They were coming up on the half-mile marker, where the horses would start their workout. Cindy could barely hold Champion back as he sensed her tension. The colt knew they were about to run. The marker shot by. "Go for it!" Cindy leaned forward, pressing her hands tight on Champion's neck.

The chestnut colt exploded into his racing gallop, his hooves churning across the track. Cindy hung on tight as Champion's mane whipped her face. Limitless dropped back by half a length as Champion powered across the muddy surface. "That's it," Cindy called. "Way to go, Champion!"

The colt responded to her voice, lengthening his strides. Cindy bent her head close to Champion's neck as they pounded into the stretch. Champion was going unbelievably fast!

Limitless is eating our mud! Cindy thought with satisfaction. She glanced back to see just how much of a lead Champion had.

Ashleigh was pulling Limitless right into Champion's flank! "No!" Cindy cried. She kneaded her hands into Champion's neck, asking for more speed—but he didn't have it on the muddy track. Panicking, Cindy checked the colt hard. Limitless swept by.

Confused and upset, Champion charged after the other colt. Instantly Cindy reacted. She had to keep control of Champion so that he didn't hurt himself or any of the other horses running on the track. And she and Champion just had to catch Limitless!

Cindy checked the colt lightly until his gallop had smoothed out again. "Now, boy—go get 'em!" she said through gritted teeth. Champion bounded along the track. Limitless had a lead of several lengths on them, but Champion was gaining with every stride.

Mud spattered Cindy's face even harder than before as Champion closed the gap to Limitless. But she didn't care about anything but the horse beneath her and speed. Champion was just behind Limitless. . . . Cindy pulled Champion to the outside to go around them. Abruptly the mud stopped hitting them. But the wire flashed overhead!

"Oh, no!" Cindy dropped her hands on Champion's neck and stood in the stirrups. She couldn't believe Limitless had just beaten her colt. *But that ride wasn't fair*, Cindy thought. *Ashleigh made Limitless interfere with us!*

Mud coated Champion's head, chest, and legs. But he stepped lightly along as Cindy walked him back to the gap, his dirty coat obviously not bothering him at all. With a sharp pang Cindy noticed how beautiful Champion was, even when he was buried in mud.

"That was a bullet work, boy!" Ashleigh praised Limitless.

"You were good, too, Champion." Cindy rubbed Champion's neck, not caring that her hand came away filthy. "It wasn't your fault Limitless got in your way!"

Ashleigh reached the gap and slipped out of the saddle. Cindy rode up behind her and dismounted, too. "What happened out there?" she asked Ashleigh, breathless. Cindy expected an apology and a long explanation from Ashleigh of how Limitless had gotten out of control.

To Cindy's astonishment, Ashleigh burst out laughing. "Good race, Cindy!" she said. "You almost caught us at the end even though I crowded you."

"You mean you did that on purpose?" Cindy couldn't believe her ears.

"I'm sorry I scared you." Ashleigh was still smiling.

That wasn't the apology Cindy was looking for. Ashleigh had almost killed Champion, and she thought it was funny?

"I wouldn't have hit you—I pulled Limitless over at the last second," Ashleigh explained.

Ashleigh can ride so precisely at that speed? Cindy's mouth dropped open. "But—you interfered with us!" Cindy was sweating and near tears from frustration.

Ashleigh looked serious. "No, I didn't, Cindy. Limitless didn't touch Champion, and I had complete control of him. I wasn't even that close to Champion—you just overreacted."

Ashleigh thinks that awful ride was my fault? Cindy

felt a sharp jolt of fear. *Now what will happen?* Ashleigh was being totally unfair, but she might not let Cindy ride in Dubai after this!

"Don't worry, Cindy. You pulled that ride out like a pro," Mike said reassuringly.

"You sure did—you rode extremely well," Ashleigh agreed quickly. "I know how much you love Champion, and you don't want him to get hurt. That's probably why you thought he was in danger. Just try to gauge the traffic better the next time you ride."

Cindy nodded, but her feelings of envy, anger, and fear were upsetting her stomach. Champion nibbled her hand, as if to give her courage. "Does this mean I can't ride Champion anymore?" Cindy finally managed to say.

Ashleigh was already talking to Ian. She looked back at Cindy. "I don't see any problems for Dubai," she said, and returned to her conversation.

I didn't have any problems, either, until now, Cindy thought. "Come on, Champion—let's get you back to the barn," she said. Cindy knew she should be grateful that Ashleigh was still letting her ride in the Dubai World Cup. But as Cindy walked Champion toward the backside, all she could think was that Ashleigh had spoiled the work in the first place. Was this what it was going to be like to compete against Ashleigh?

Champion bumped her from behind, and Cindy turned to see what he wanted. She had to smile a little at the soft, happy expression in her beloved colt's dark eyes. "You don't know what's wrong, do you?" she asked. "As long as we're together, you're happy." Cindy tickled the colt's snip on the end of his nose. "You're right, boy—that's what's important. Together we can do anything, even win the Dubai World Cup. Even Ashleigh can't beat us."

The big colt nudged her fondly again, as if to say he'd always be on her side.

13

"LOOK AT THIS PLACE!" CINDY EXCLAIMED FOUR DAYS LATER as she walked off the plane in the United Arab Emirates. Cindy could hardly believe she was halfway around the world, in the desert birthplace of Arabian horses, the ancestors of Thoroughbreds.

The sky, a vast stretch of brilliant blue, hung over the endless, rippling sands of the desert. Cindy could see the modern skyscrapers of the city of Dubai, stark white against the sky. A clean, hot wind swept across the airport tarmac.

Ashleigh stretched her arms over her head and yawned. Cindy rubbed a crick in her back. They had been traveling for an extremely long time.

In the distance Cindy saw a train of camels slowly making their way across the dunes. She remembered reading that a camel-racing track was nearby.

She tried to imagine racing on one of those long-legged, spindly camels, balancing behind the hump, but she couldn't. *There must be some trick to it I don't know about*, she thought.

She looked up at the plane. Both Champion and Limitless were aboard. "I hope Champion's okay," she said anxiously. Cindy had last seen Champion in Amsterdam, the rest stop in the six-thousand-mile trip from the United States.

First Cindy, Mike, Ian, and Ashleigh had driven both Champion and Limitless to Atlanta, Georgia. Beth planned to stay home with Kevin and Christina and catch the race on TV. Vic and Mark had followed in Vic's car. In Atlanta the colts had been loaded into stalls in the cargo section of the plane while the Whitebrook people sat up front. The plane had flown to Amsterdam and stopped to give the horses a few hours' break.

At the rest stop Champion, clearly bored with being kept in close quarters for so long, had plunged around the small pen supplied for the two colts to stretch their legs. Cindy had watched him nervously. She had wondered what she would do if Champion escaped and ran off into Holland.

Champion was probably much more unhappy by

now, after another eight or nine hours on the plane. Cindy walked over to the cargo ramp and gazed up, trying to see him.

Limitless stepped onto the ramp, following Vic. The bay colt snorted softly at the strange surroundings. "It's all right, boy." Ashleigh went quickly to the colt's head. "I know—everything looks pretty strange here after Florida!"

Champion whinnied shrilly. Cindy saw the showy colt poised at the top of the ramp. "Come on, Champion!" she called. "Welcome to Dubai!"

The dark chestnut colt pranced off the plane, following Ian and Mike. At the bottom of the ramp he stopped short and whinnied loudly again, as if to greet his ancestral homeland. Several men who were waiting to greet the plane smiled approvingly. They wore *kandoras*, the traditional white robelike dress of the United Arab Emirates, and *ghutras*, flowing sheet-like headgear secured by a black band.

"You ham, Champion," Cindy said with a laugh.

Champion's head jerked around at the sound of her voice. Pulling Ian and Mike behind him, the colt trotted over to Cindy.

"Hello to you, too." Cindy hugged Champion's glossy neck. She was glad the colt seemed to like this new country.

"Let's get them settled in at the track," Ashleigh said, leading Limitless into a waiting horse van.

Champion bounded in after the other colt, as if he couldn't wait to see his temporary home.

On the drive to the track Cindy and Ashleigh sat together in the backseat while Ian and Mike rode up front with the driver. Vic and Mark followed in a second car.

Cindy couldn't take her eyes off their driver, who had a hooded falcon perched on his arm. "What's the falcon for?" she asked, leaning forward.

The driver shrugged, then smiled. "I use him for hunting—but right now he's just along for the ride."

"Oh." Cindy sat back. That seemed strange. But the more she thought about it, the more sense it made. *I'd probably take Champion everywhere if he'd fit in a car*, she thought.

"Look over there, Cindy." Ian pointed to the smooth dome and tall minaret, or tower, of a mosque, the Moslem place of worship. Islam was the Arabic religion.

Cindy stared at the massive mosque and delicate spire of the minaret. The mosque looked nothing like an American church to her—its domelike shape looked more like the Jefferson Memorial in Washington. But the stately grandeur of the building signified its higher purpose.

As Cindy looked out the window, she could see that alongside the road there was a large canal that flowed with stunning, deep blue water. *Dhows*, flat wooden boats that looked like big rowboats, cruised the water peacefully alongside modern yachts.

"That's Dubai Creek," Ashleigh said, consulting her guidebook.

Cindy nodded. She was glad Ashleigh was talking to her. Ashleigh hadn't exactly been unfriendly for the past few days, since they'd worked Limitless and Champion together, but she hadn't said much, either. And she hadn't suggested that they work the colts together again. Cindy wondered if she would here in Dubai.

"We'll need to work the horses once at night, won't we?" Cindy asked.

"That's right. We have to get them used to the floodlights since the race is at night," Ian replied. "But we'll work out the details later."

"There's the track!" Cindy said excitedly. To her left, the inner turf course and center island of the Nad Al Sheba track was a startling oasis of lush green against the tawny sands of the desert. The brilliant white stands behind the track looked like a distant mirage. Up ahead was the stable block for the overseas horses.

Cindy jumped out of the car as soon as it stopped and waited impatiently for the van to arrive with Champion and Limitless. The stable block consisted of four barns, one barn for the horses from each continent. In the middle of the complex was a cross-shaped building where the grooms would stay.

"Dad, can I stay here with the horses?" Cindy asked.

Ian laughed. "No, the owners, trainers, and jockeys are staying at the Forte Grand Jumeirah Beach, a five-star hotel. I think you'll be happy there, honey."

"I guess." Cindy decided to see if Champion seemed okay in the new barn. If he needed her, she would just have to stay.

The van pulled up into the stable yard, and Cindy walked over to meet it, her shoes sinking deep in the hot sand. Vic dropped the tailgate to the van and carefully backed Champion down the ramp.

"This is home for now, boy," Cindy said, going to the colt's head and leading him toward the barn. Ian followed her, and Mike and Ashleigh led Limitless into the barn.

Champion's eyes were bright and interested as he took in his new surroundings. The barn was spotlessly painted white, with tall, airy ceilings. Not a splinter of hay was out of place.

Champion stopped in front of his stall. His ears pricked at the sound of a horse stamping impatiently. Two stalls down a beautiful gray colt was watching them over his half door. Cindy gasped. "He looks just like Glory!"

"Well, it's not too surprising that Just Deserts looks like Glory since they have the same grandsire," said a familiar voice behind her.

Cindy whirled. "Ben, hi!" She hadn't seen Glory's

first trainer in a long time. She eased Champion into his stall and closed the door. Then she gave Ben a warm hug hello.

"How have you been, Ben?" Ashleigh asked, coming from Limitless's stall. She shook hands with the older trainer. Mike and Ian stepped forward to greet Ben as well.

"Just fine, thanks. I don't need to ask how you've been, with a Triple Crown winner at Whitebrook," Ben said with a laugh.

Cindy couldn't take her eyes off the gray colt. *He looks like he's got every bit of Glory's power*, she thought.

"It's a shame Just Deserts missed the Triple Crown," Ian said.

"Yes, he set a track record in the Jim Beam just before the Kentucky Derby, but he injured himself," Ben replied. "I didn't want to risk running him last spring or summer."

"Running so hard that he got hurt sounds like something Champion or Glory would do," Cindy said. She was sure Just Deserts would be a tough contender in the Dubai race.

"He's got a lot of heart," Ben agreed. He smiled at Cindy. "I'd like to show you another horse, if you have time. I think you'll enjoy seeing him. But he's at another stable."

"Sure," Cindy said, intrigued. Ben was always full of surprises. "Is it okay if I go with Ben, Dad?" she asked.

"Sure," Ian replied. "We'll get settled in at our hotel."

"I'd like to come, too, if that's okay with you, Ben," Ashleigh said.

"I was just going to suggest it," Ben told her.

Cindy looked uncertainly at Champion. "I wonder if he'll be okay while I'm gone." The big colt was eyeing Just Deserts and nibbling a bit of hay from his net. He seemed content.

"Mark and Vic will watch him," Ian answered. "They're getting settled into their rooms, but they'll be here in a minute."

"We won't be long," Ben promised.

"Okay," Cindy agreed. She and Ashleigh then followed Ben to his car.

Cindy settled back in her seat to enjoy the ride and Ben's company. Vast expanses of flat desert rolled by, unbroken by any sign of life. Cindy wondered where they were going, but she knew better than to ask. Ben liked his surprises to be complete. *Well, this horse can't be too far away,* she thought. The United Arab Emirates was a small country. Before long they would run into the sea, the vast Persian Gulf.

"How has Just Deserts been training?" Ashleigh asked.

"Very well," Ben said. "He's been here for over a month. He seems to be taking to the track surface— his timings are good."

Ashleigh nodded. "We'll see how our horses do. How did you get Just Deserts used to the surface?"

"Don't forget we're the competition, Ben," Cindy said. She hoped Ben wasn't offended by Ashleigh's questions.

"Oh, I don't think I'm giving anything away." Ben smiled. "Just because I tell you my strategy doesn't mean you'll know how to use it. In answer to your question, Ashleigh, I've simply been giving him a lot of exercise on the track. His improved clockings have shown that he's getting used to it."

"How do you think Champion will do on the track, Ashleigh?" Cindy asked.

"I'm not sure." Ashleigh looked out the window.

Cindy's face burned with embarrassment. *Why isn't she talking to me again?* she wondered. *She has plenty to say to Ben!* Ben was silent, too, apparently sensing the tension in the car. Cindy sat up straight. Suddenly she knew why Ashleigh didn't want to talk to her about training anymore. Ashleigh was afraid she'd lose the race if she gave Cindy tips!

Well, that's all right with me, Cindy thought, crossing her arms and looking out her own window. *I don't need Ashleigh's help—I'll figure things out for myself.*

Ben stopped the car in front of three low white buildings with red tile roofs. To the left was a patch of green grass with a strip of water in the middle. Cindy recognized it as an exercise pool for horses. Behind the buildings was a training track, a deeper shade of brown against the light sand of the surrounding desert. "Where are we?" Cindy asked.

"You'll know in a minute." Ben was already walking into the building on the far right. Cindy heard a whinny and a couple of nickers. Clearly the building was a stable.

Cindy looked at Ashleigh and shrugged. Ashleigh smiled, lifted her hands in an oh-well gesture, and followed Ben into the barn.

Cindy sighed. For just a second she'd felt close to Ashleigh again. *I wish things weren't so bad between us*, Cindy thought sadly as she walked into the barn. The stalls were painted white, with black half doors. Looking over the doors was a rainbow of exquisite Thoroughbreds: blacks, bays, grays, and chestnuts. Their lovely heads and intelligent expressions bespoke their fine breeding.

Cindy drew in a quick, appreciative breath. She was sure that wherever this was, it was one of the finest stables in the world.

"Here comes an old friend," Ben said.

Cindy turned quickly at the sound of a horse's hooves. In front of her stood a majestic dark chestnut colt, almost the color of Champion, with a perfect diamond on his forehead. The colt was even more beautiful than the other horses in the stable. "Wow," she gasped. "Who's this?"

"Don't you know Clover?" asked the man leading him. He was in his thirties and wore traditional Arabic dress. Cindy recognized him from his pictures in racing magazines as Humaid Obaid, a trainer at Sheikh Hassan Al Taleb's Byerly Stables.

Cindy's heart began to beat a little faster. *So that's where we are*, she thought. *We are at one of the world's best stables!* "How could I ever forget Clover?" she asked. Four Leaf Clover was one of the orphan foals she had helped to raise when she first came to Whitebrook. He had been sold to an Arabian stable two and a half years ago at the Keeneland select yearling sale. Cindy had tried not to think about him. She had been badly hurt when the colt was sold so far away, and she had thought she'd never see him again. "That's him?" she asked in wonder.

"His name is now Al Sha'ar," said the trainer. "That means 'the poet.'"

"I've read about him. I didn't realize Al Sha'ar was you, Clover!" Cindy stepped eagerly toward the colt. She loved his new name. "You've gotten so big and beautiful!"

The colt shifted restlessly and lowered his head to look at her.

"You don't remember me," Cindy said, feeling a pang. She remembered all the hours she had spent teaching the colt his manners before the September select yearling sale at Saratoga.

"Come closer," said the trainer. "See if he remembers your scent."

Cindy stepped up to the colt and held out her hand. "It's me, boy," she whispered.

Al Sha'ar dropped his lovely head and delicately sniffed her hand. Cindy held her breath. The colt's dark eyes were questioning. Slowly he lowered his head even more . . . and checked her right-front jeans pocket for a carrot.

"You do remember!" Cindy cried. The big colt contentedly nudged her pocket, as if they'd seen each other yesterday instead of years before.

"Al Sha'ar has won several grade-one races in Britain and France for our stable," said Humaid Obaid. There was no mistaking the pride in the trainer's voice.

"He's a good horse," Ashleigh said, smiling. "We know that, don't we, Cindy?"

"Sure." Cindy was glad to see that Clover had done so well. With his long, arched neck and delicate, refined head, he really looked like an Arabian.

"I'm actually here to extend an invitation," the trainer said. "Sheikh Hassan Al Taleb would be most honored if both you, Ben, and the group from Whitebrook would join him this evening for dinner."

"I don't want to leave Champion for so long," Cindy said quickly, then bit her lip. She didn't want to seem rude.

"You would all be welcome," the trainer assured her. "Including Champion. I do understand your concern. We Arabs like our horses to be with us also."

"We'd love to come," Ashleigh said.

"About seven, then?" asked the trainer. "The sheikh has a beautiful house and grounds, but I think tonight we will go out into the desert."

Cindy smiled, barely able to contain her excitement. *This is going to be a real Arabian night out of my dreams!* she thought.

That evening the stars glittered brightly in the black velvet night and a soft, hot wind blew off the desert. Cindy sat on a velvet pillow near the fire, holding Champion on a lead line. She had just finished a meal of lamb and rice, flavored with strong, delicious spices and served with soft, warm bread.

Cindy turned to hand Champion a date, part of her dessert of assorted fruits. She had just discovered that the colt liked dates as much as oranges.

Champion looks so gorgeous, Cindy thought. The firelight flickered in a thousand dark flames off the colt's mahogany coat, and tiny orange flames gleamed in his almost black eyes. Champion seemed like a mystery horse in the desert, so far from home. He nudged Cindy gently, and she lifted a hand to stroke his nose.

Cindy gazed out into the desert, unable to see anything beyond the sea of dunes. She heard the whisper of the sand, almost like the soft sound of a voice, as the dunes endlessly reshaped themselves. *I wonder what Max is doing,* Cindy thought. *It would be so romantic if he could be here with me.* She imagined kissing Max under the bright, unfamiliar stars, and the warmth and safety of Max's arms holding her in a tight embrace.

"What's the matter?" Ben asked quietly. He sat beside Cindy, finishing a honey-sweetened pastry.

"Oh, I miss my boyfriend." Cindy glanced at Ben. "Does that sound childish?"

"Not at all," Ben replied. "It's part of missing home, and I think we all do. I miss my wife."

Cindy looked across the fire. Ashleigh was sitting on the other side, talking quietly to Mike, Ian, Sheikh Hassan Al Taleb, and Humaid Obaid. They were sipping *gahwa,* the traditional Arabic coffee, and the rich, aromatic smell wafted to Cindy's nose. Ashleigh held Limitless Time's lead rope. Cindy smiled at how close Limitless was standing to Ashleigh. The brown colt could take part in the conversation if he chose.

Humaid Obaid stood up. "There is just enough moonlight to see by," he said. "Shall we go for a ride? Myself on Al Sha'ar, Ben on Just Deserts, Ashleigh on Limitless Time, and Cindy on Champion. I brought saddles and bridles for all the horses."

174

Cindy stared at him in amazement. "I'd love to!" The moon was just rising over the sloping peaks of the dunes, bathing them in pale white light. Cindy had never imagined she'd be going for a ride across the moonlit desert with three of the greatest race-horses in the world! "May I, Dad?"

Ian nodded. "But stay with the other riders. It would be easy to get lost out there—all the dunes look pretty much the same."

"I will." Cindy was already leading Champion to the sheikh's trailer to tack the colt up. She doubted if Champion would get lost, but she intended to be careful anyway.

"Ready?" Ashleigh asked minutes later. She was on Limitless, waiting with the other two riders behind the four-wheel-drive vehicles that had brought them into the desert.

"Let's go," Cindy said, sitting comfortably in Champion's saddle. Champion confidently stepped off ahead of the other horses and plunged up a steep dune. He was laboring a bit in the deep sand, Cindy noticed. But he seemed not to mind the difficult foot-ing or the unusual landscape.

It's almost as if he's been here before, Cindy thought as she stopped him at the top of the dune to wait for Ashleigh, Ben, and Humaid Obaid. *Does Champion somehow know this is where his ancestors came from?*

A stiff wind blew grains of sand into Cindy's face.

Under the bright moonlight towering dunes and rippling sand seas stretched everywhere she looked. Cindy imagined herself in the time a thousand years ago, when everybody had gorgeous horses like these and rode through the desert.

"I'll lead the way," said Humaid Obaid. The Arabian trainer and Ben dropped over the far side of the dune on Al Sha'ar and Just Deserts.

Cindy waited to ride with Ashleigh. Cindy didn't have Max to confide in, but maybe she could share some of her feelings about this wonderful night with Ashleigh. They'd had some misunderstandings lately, but usually Ashleigh was very sensitive.

"Cindy, Champion's really floundering in the sand," Ashleigh said with a frown as she stopped Limitless Time. "That worries me. I wonder how he'll do on the sandy track at Nad al Sheba. Of course, this sand is much looser than the track surface, but still . . ."

Cindy felt as if Ashleigh had just burst her magic bubble. *Now she gives me a training tip, just when I don't want one,* Cindy thought. *And anyway, she's totally wrong about how Champion is handling the surface.* Cindy nudged Champion with her heels to speed him up so that she wouldn't have to talk to Ashleigh. She really didn't trust herself to make a civil reply.

"Wait, Cindy," Ashleigh called. But Cindy trotted Champion down the backside of a dune, forgetting her promise to stay with the other horses. She had to get out of earshot.

"If I listen to Ashleigh, I'm going to lose my concentration for the Dubai race, just like I did in my first race," Cindy told herself grimly. "I'll find out how Champion handles sand on the track, all right—but it's not going to be when Ashleigh's around."

14

THREE NIGHTS LATER CINDY SLIPPED OUT OF HER BED IN THE grooms' quarters at the stable block and peered out the window. The full moon shone brightly on the barns, the track, and the vast desert beyond. The stable yard was deserted. "Good, no one will see me take out Champion," Cindy whispered. She hadn't really expected anyone to be stirring at two in the morning.

Cindy felt a stab of guilt as she hurried across the stable yard to get Champion. Cindy had told her dad that she needed to stay in the grooms' quarters with Champion, instead of at the hotel, to keep the colt quiet. Ian, Ashleigh, and Mike had praised

Cindy's decision to give up staying at the luxurious beach resort for Champion's good.

Well, Champion does need me, Cindy defended herself as she stepped inside the barn. *Just not quite the way Dad and the rest of them think.*

Cindy jumped at the sound of a soft rustle near the barn. "Who's there?" she whispered, her heart pounding.

The sound came again, and Cindy realized it was just the wind blowing the fronds of a nearby palm tree. *Calm down*, she ordered herself. *You'll make Champion nervous, too.*

Cindy tiptoed to Champion's stall, guided by the soft glow of the night-lights. All the horses seemed to be asleep.

Suddenly Champion popped his head over his stall half door and nickered. Cindy was so startled, she almost screamed. "Hi, boy," she gasped. "Let's get you ready."

Champion fidgeted while Cindy brushed him and tacked him up. The change in his routine might be making him nervous. *I have to do this*, she reminded herself.

"Come on, Champion," she whispered, leading him to the doorway.

A light flicked on at the opposite end of the barn. Cindy's heart caught in her throat.

"Cindy?" Mark said, walking down the aisle.

"Oh, it's just you." Cindy sighed with relief. "You scared me to death."

"What are you doing?" Mark pointed to Champion.

Cindy thought fast. She'd have to tell Mark what she was doing—there was no other possible explanation why Champion was tacked up. "I'm taking Champion out on the track," she said.

"Alone, at two in the morning?" Mark stared at her in disbelief. "Cindy, you've totally lost it."

"Don't try to stop me," Cindy warned, pulling Champion onto the path to the track. The colt spooked when he saw his black shadow against the pale sand. Cindy waited while Champion figured out what the shadow was, although her pulse raced at the delay.

"I'm definitely going to stop you if you don't tell me why you're doing this without telling anyone," Mark said.

"Mark, I have to." Cindy prayed he wouldn't call her dad. Wasn't Mark her friend?

A quick breeze picked up, scattering fine sand across the path. Champion skittered sideways, tossing his head.

"He's getting upset," Mark said.

"It's your fault," Cindy snapped. She had to get rid of Mark before he ruined her whole plan.

Mark looked at her skeptically. "You're telling me

180

you have to take Champion out alone, which is breaking the rules, and you have to do it without telling anyone—which is also against the rules?"

"That's right, but I have my reasons. Champion's been out on the track a couple of times since we got to Dubai," Cindy said, forcing herself to speak slowly so that Mark could understand. "He does seem to be having a little trouble handling the surface, but not nearly as much as everyone thinks. So Dad and Ashleigh aren't letting me gallop him as fast as he should be."

"Oh, really." Mark snorted. "So you think you can just take Champion out tonight against their advice?"

"Doesn't anyone trust me?" Cindy asked desperately. "I know what I'm doing!"

Mark looked at her for several moments. "I can't stop you from taking him out there," he said. "But think about it, Cindy." Mark began walking back to the stable block.

"I've thought about it plenty," Cindy whispered, but he was already out of earshot. *Just forget about him*, she ordered herself. *Pay attention.*

The lights of Dubai twinkled in the distance as Cindy mounted up at the gap to the track. She didn't have a mounting block, so she jumped from the outside rail onto Champion's back.

The moment she landed, she realized her mistake.

Champion wasn't used to being mounted that way. The colt shied and half reared as her unbalanced weight shifted on his back. "Whoa, boy!" Cindy cried, grabbing his mane to keep from falling.

The colt came down on all fours, trembling. Cindy quickly nudged him forward with her heels, asking for a walk. Instead Champion broke into a short-striding gallop, tugging hard on the reins. Cindy immediately pulled him down into an uneven, forced trot.

She let out a sigh of frustration. "This isn't going to work at all, boy," she murmured. "I'll just take you back to the barn."

As if he understood that his ordeal would soon end, Champion trotted almost evenly around the track. Cindy couldn't wait to reach the gap so that she could get off, and this disastrous ride would be over.

Cindy started with fright when she saw three still, silent black figures standing at the gap. "Oh, God." Cindy's spirits plummeted. It was her dad, Ashleigh, and Mark.

"Get off that horse this instant," Ian said as Cindy approached. His tone was quiet, but Cindy had never seen him angrier. She quickly dismounted.

"Cindy, I'm sorry I told them." Mark looked upset. "But I was afraid you'd get hurt."

Cindy didn't reply. Her hands were shaking so

much, she could hardly hold Champion's reins. *What are they going to do to me?* she thought miserably.

"Give the horse to Mark," Ian ordered. "Mark, please take Champion back to the barn. We'll be there in a minute to check him over."

Cindy handed Champion's reins to Mark. Champion looked at Cindy, then nudged her. He didn't seem to understand why he wasn't going with her.

"It's okay, boy," Cindy choked out. Champion still wanted to be with her, even after the way she'd frightened him. He was her only friend in this crowd. And he was such a good one, she realized. *How could I have put him in danger like that?* she thought. *I love him so much.*

"Come on, boy," Mark said, tugging on Champion's reins. The colt finally followed him at his usual brisk, lively walk.

"Well, Cindy?" Ian folded his arms. "What were you doing out there?"

Cindy's lips trembled, but she forced herself to speak. She had to try to explain. "I wanted to take Champion a little faster on the track than we had been just to see how he'd handle it," she said.

Ian stared at her. His expression was such a mix of anger, disbelief, and disappointment that Cindy's knees felt weak. She gripped the rail to support herself. Her dad was really, really mad. Cindy didn't even dare look at Ashleigh. *They can't take me off Champion in the race this late, can they?* she wondered frantically.

The silence was deafening. Cindy bit her lip and stared at the ground.

"Cindy, Ashleigh and I had planned to breeze Champion tomorrow," Ian finally said. "But instead you risked life and limb—yours and Champion's—to come out here tonight, for absolutely no purpose. What got into you? You've run around tonight as if you were an irresponsible child. I thought we could start treating you like an adult."

"You haven't been!" Cindy bit back a cry. "Champion's my horse, but nobody cares what I think about his training! You treat me like a big baby all the time!"

"Champion isn't your horse." Ashleigh's tone was clipped.

"He is too!" Cindy screamed. "Just because you own him—"

"I didn't mean that," Ashleigh interrupted. "You don't understand. And keep your voice down."

"Go back to the stable block, Cindy." Ian sounded weary. "I'll drive you to the hotel after I take care of Champion. Obviously you can't be left here alone."

Cindy looked from her dad to Ashleigh, trying to find some trace of sympathy in their faces. She saw none. Maybe she could put things right if she apologized. "I—I'm sorry," she stammered.

Ashleigh turned away. "I've never been so disappointed in anyone," she said coldly. "Don't talk to me, Cindy."

"Oh, Max—I'm so glad you're home," Cindy cried into the phone. "Everything is going wrong." Cindy looked over her shoulder to see if her dad had come up from the barn to her room in the grooms' quarters. All she needed now was to have him catch her making a phone call from the United Arab Emirates to the United States.

"What's the matter?" Max's voice was worried. "You sound terrible."

"I think it's safe to say that everything is the matter." Cindy drew a deep breath and quickly filled Max in on what had happened. "The worst part was when Ashleigh said Champion isn't my horse," she finished. "Max, Ashleigh just *hates* me. I mean, things were bad between us before, but now . . ." Cindy shuddered as she remembered the contempt in Ashleigh's voice.

"Cindy, I think you're blowing this out of proportion," Max said soothingly.

"You weren't there." Cindy sniffed and wiped her nose.

"No, I meant this whole thing with Ashleigh," Max said. "About who's going to win the race."

"What could be more important than that?" Cindy rummaged in her jeans pocket for a tissue. She couldn't find one.

Max cleared his throat. "Look, Cindy, I *don't* know if you can beat Ashleigh," he said.

"What do you mean?" Cindy wailed, stamping her foot. How could Max start in on her, too?

"She's got a lot more experience than you do," Max said quickly. "Why not face reality? She may win. But why do you care so much?"

Cindy felt too worn out to be mad at Max. "I just do," she said, her voice thick.

"You don't have to beat her to be a good jockey," Max went on. "If Ashleigh wasn't in the race at all, would you really do anything differently?"

"No, I guess not," Cindy said slowly. "But Max, Ashleigh is just as competitive about the race as I am. You wouldn't believe how mean she was to me tonight."

"I think you just scared her by taking out Champion," Max said. "She probably almost had a heart attack when she saw you on the track."

"Huh." Cindy tried to put herself in Ashleigh's shoes. After a few moments she sighed heavily. She supposed Ashleigh *did* have a right to be frightened and angry when she saw Cindy and Champion on the track.

"And what if you ride him in the race that way?" Max asked.

"What way? I don't know what you're talking about." Cindy was so tired and stressed, she could barely think.

"Like you don't care about him but just about winning," Max said softly.

"But I don't just care about winning!" Cindy burst out. "I just want to beat Ashleigh in the Dubai race so that people will take me seriously as a jockey."

"They do already, or you wouldn't be there," Max pointed out. "You know that."

"Well . . . yeah." *So what have I got left to prove?* Cindy wondered. *I guess . . . just that Champion and I can do our best together. That I won't let him down, the way I did tonight.*

Cindy stifled a yawn. She felt much too tired to figure this all out now.

"Get some sleep," Max advised. "Everything will look better in the morning."

"Maybe." Cindy hesitated. "Max, I miss you so much."

"Same here. Good luck, Cindy."

Cindy knew he meant with more than the race. "Thanks," she said. "I'll call you really soon."

Cindy sighed as she hung up. She hated to let Max go. "I wish I were home," she whispered.

Well, you aren't. Cindy forced herself to stand up

straight. She couldn't give up now. Before she went home, she had to ride the best race of her life—and make it up to her dad and Ashleigh for what she'd done tonight.

Maybe Max is right about Ashleigh, Cindy thought. *But how can I ever face her again?*

The next morning Cindy flopped down on a bench in front of the Forte Grand Jumeirah Beach hotel. She felt strange sitting at a five-star hotel in disgrace, but Cindy had no doubt that was the case. This morning no one had woken her to go to the track, and Cindy had been so tired from last night, she'd overslept. Ian, Ashleigh, and Mike had all left without her. Cindy was afraid to think what that meant for her ride in the Dubai World Cup.

"Good morning, Cindy." Ben sat down beside her. "Beautiful day, isn't it?"

"I guess every day is beautiful around here. For everyone but me." Cindy stared unhappily at the lovely beach, where quiet waves lapped miles of smooth white sand. Ordinarily Cindy would have loved to walk on the deserted beach or swim in the clear blue-green waters of the Gulf. But today she felt too depressed to do anything.

"Mark told me about your little escapade last night," Ben said.

"Mark has a big mouth." Cindy wrapped her arms around her knees.

"You can't really blame Ian and Ashleigh for being upset," Ben said. "They're Champion's trainers. And you broke their trust in you."

"But I didn't mean to." Cindy felt sick. Because of that one mistake, she almost certainly wouldn't be riding Champion in the race. "I guess I stopped listening to my dad and Ashleigh," she added. "All they do is criticize and boss me around for no reason."

"They have a big reason—they've got so much confidence in you," Ben said. "They wouldn't bother to give you advice if they didn't think you were worth it."

"Do you think so?" Cindy asked in surprise.

"Of course. But Cindy, you've got to listen to that advice. Ashleigh and your dad are smart people who have your best interests at heart. Don't take advice as a slight to your self-esteem. You've got to have faith in yourself."

"You're right." Cindy let out a breath, feeling her anger slowly slip away. She smiled ruefully. "I just wish you'd told me all this before I lost my chance to ride in the race."

Ben looked surprised. "What makes you think you won't be riding?" he asked.

Cindy shrugged. "Dad and Ashleigh left me here this morning."

"They went on a tour of some neighboring stables, but they're coming back for you this evening," Ben said. "You're going to ride Champion under the floodlights at the track to get him used to them. It's close to race time."

15

"RIDERS UP!" THE PADDOCK JUDGE CALLED. IN JUST FIFTEEN minutes the Dubai World Cup was scheduled to go off.

Cindy's stomach fluttered. *This is really it*, she thought. Cindy stood at the side of the walking ring, watching the nine gorgeous Thoroughbreds who were to challenge for the richest race in the world and the title of world champion.

All the horses looked fit and ready, but none was so beautiful as Champion, Cindy thought. The dark chestnut colt was marching energetically after Ian, his eyes gleaming as he took in the other horses, the brilliant lights on the nighttime track, and the hordes of spectators, many of them in white Arabic dress.

"Here he is," Ian said, leading Champion over to Cindy.

"Hi, big guy." Cindy took Champion's head between her hands. She felt a surge of confidence just being near the lovely colt. Champion's muscles were taut and toned over his neck, shoulders, and hindquarters. The light bounced off his chocolate-colored coat in winking, shimmering kisses.

Champion whinnied a little and pranced in place, as if to say, I'm ready!

"Me too." Cindy patted the big colt's glossy shoulder. Cindy knew she'd prepared him the best she could. The colt's work on the track under the floodlights had been first rate. He hadn't seemed afraid of shadows, and his time had been excellent.

Cindy saw Mike take Limitless over to Ashleigh. The older jockey had started being civil to Cindy again, but Cindy knew that Ashleigh still wasn't really talking to her.

I'd be so happy now if Ashleigh wasn't mad at me, Cindy thought. She hated to race against Ashleigh when they were enemies. Cindy had missed Ashleigh over the past week—her advice, her humor, and the support that Cindy now realized had always been there. Ian had forgiven Cindy for taking Champion to the track without permission, but Cindy was sure Ashleigh hadn't.

Ian gave Cindy a leg into the saddle. "Remember what we talked about. Go straight to the lead if you can, but try to rate Champion if there's too much early speed. Arabesque from France may push the pace. Champion will need to save something for the stretch—it's three furlongs, remember, not a quarter mile like most tracks."

Cindy nodded. As usual, she knew all the facts about the track and the horses in the field.

"Just Deserts has some of that same fire and talent that Glory does, and he's a real stayer," Ian continued. "And this is Al Sha'ar's home—he should do well on the sand. Limitless is one of the best closers in the world. He'll be there in the end. But we'll have to see how the race plays out."

"Got it." Cindy tightened the strap on her helmet. *If there's one sure thing in racing, it's that a race never plays out quite like you expect*, she thought.

"You're all set, sweetheart." Ian patted her boot. "Go for it."

"I will." Cindy gathered her reins and drew a deep breath as she looked toward the track. "Okay, Champion—let's do it."

As Champion stepped off on the rubber path to the track Cindy mentally prepared herself. She was under no illusions that the race would be easy or that her natural talent would win it for her. *I've got to stay focused on what I'm doing*, she reminded herself. *That's helping Champion run the best race he possibly can.*

Limitless Time stood quietly while Mike and Ashleigh conferred about the race. The bay colt was in peak condition, and Ashleigh looked relaxed but professional.

Cindy's heart ached. She would have liked to speak to Ashleigh for just a moment before the race. *But maybe that wouldn't be right*, she thought.

Andrea Devons, the jockey of Chivalrous Knight, a colt from Great Britain, gave Cindy a scornful look as she rode by on her way to the track. Cindy returned her stare. She'd already taken some heat from the other jockeys in the race about her inexperience. *I don't care what you have to say*, she thought defiantly.

Andrea turned her mount toward the track. "Don't fall off in the post parade, Cindy," she said.

"I won't—don't choke on the dirt Champion throws back in your face," Cindy retorted. The other jockey shot her an angry look, but she rode off without another word.

"Cindy!" Ashleigh called, walking over on Limitless.

Cindy looked back and stopped Champion. What did Ashleigh want? Cindy prayed Ashleigh wouldn't say anything too bad. *I just couldn't take it before the race*, she thought.

Ashleigh laughed. "You seem to be handling the prerace jitters pretty well."

"I guess so." Cindy smiled back. For a moment it seemed like old times. "Ashleigh . . ." Cindy hesitated. "I really am so sorry about what happened with Champion that night."

"And I'm sorry I didn't accept your apology the first time." Ashleigh shifted in the saddle on Limitless. The two colts stood quietly next to each other, as if they were buddies instead of rivals. "I do want to clear something up."

"What's that?" Cindy was so relieved to be really talking to Ashleigh again, she almost didn't care what Ashleigh said.

"When I said that Champion wasn't yours, I didn't mean it the way you thought," Ashleigh said. "I'm not concerned about who technically owns him. But you seemed so careless with him that night, I really felt he wasn't yours."

"I think I understand now," Cindy said shyly. "I wanted to tell you something, too. I've really missed getting your advice about training. I know I don't have enough experience to make all the decisions about Champion myself."

Ashleigh looked surprised. "You seemed so angry with me, Cindy, I really wasn't sure if I should try to talk to you." She smiled. "Besides, you're a great rider. I don't have a lot to say to you about how you should ride. And lately I haven't been in a position to give out much advice. Believe it or not, I have to concentrate on my own race."

Cindy sighed with relief. "Well, I'm glad that's settled."

"Me too. We'd better get out there. I just wanted to say good luck." Ashleigh's look was gentle and understanding.

"Thanks—same to you," Cindy said, and she meant it.

"May the best horse win." Ashleigh touched her crop to her helmet, then moved Limitless off toward the track.

Champion walked a few steps, then stopped to get his bearings. The colt flung up his statuesque head.

"You look like an Arabian," Cindy murmured. A quick thrill of excitement chased through her body. *We're going to run like the wind!* she thought.

Champion had drawn the number-three post. "Don't forget to watch out for Arabesque in the five position," Cindy whispered to herself as Champion loaded in the gate. The dapple gray colt would almost surely try to cut across the track to take the early lead.

Limitless had drawn the eight position, far to the outside. Just Deserts and Al Sha'ar flanked Champion in the two and four positions.

Chivalrous Knight had the advantage in the one position, closest to the rail. *He's a turf horse, but that position might be enough of an edge for him to be in contention,* Cindy thought. *This is a tough field any way I look at it!* She leaned over Champion's neck and wrapped her hands in the colt's dark mane, bracing herself against the shock of the break from the gate.

The gates slammed open, and the force of Champion's terrific lunge threw Cindy backward. She recovered quickly, rising over Champion's neck again.

"Al Sha'ar is off to an early lead," the announcer called. "Then it's Wonder's Champion and Arabesque; back two to Chivalrous Knight and Just Deserts. Limitless Time stumbled leaving the gate and is in sixth. . . ."

Al Sha'ar got off faster than Champion because this is his home track, Cindy thought, but her mind was already on her next move. Arabesque was cutting them off! The colt's jockey pointed him at a small opening on the rail.

Cindy felt a flash of panic. *He's too close to us— we've got to get out of the way!* she cried silently. Cindy's hands clutched reflexively at the reins to check Champion, but she forced herself to look again at Arabesque. No, the colt had room, if just barely!

"And Arabesque takes a short lead," called the announcer. "Back two to Al Sha'ar; Wonder's Champion is settled in third."

Champion wasn't settled. The colt was running easily, but he was unhappy behind the other horses. Cindy's arms already ached from trying to hold him back. Cindy wasn't sure how long she could keep it up.

Cindy quickly glanced around. Where was Limitless? *If you don't know, don't worry about it,* flashed through her mind.

She let Champion out a notch so that he was lying just off the front-runners. Arabesque was dropping back, and Al Sha'ar had taken the lead, saving ground along the rail.

Suddenly Chivalrous Knight pulled even with Al Sha'ar. Al Sha'ar fought back! As the horses pounded into the backstretch Cindy waited for either of the two front-runners to fade, but the two colts continued to battle for the lead. Catching their excitement, Champion pulled even harder on the reins.

"No, Champion! This pace is blistering—save something for the stretch!" Cindy called.

Just when Cindy was sure her tired arms couldn't hold Champion an instant longer, Chivalrous Knight dropped off the pace. He backed up so quickly, Champion almost ran into him. Cindy felt Champion's weight shift as the colt slowed. Instantly he changed to his right lead, then back to his left again. The next second Al Sha'ar dropped back. Champion was on the lead as they headed into the stretch!

"It's Wonder's Champion by half a length, with Limitless Time up close to the pace today," the announcer said. "But here comes Just Deserts!"

It's time for the closers! Cindy let Champion out another notch. The colt's snorts came quickly as he fought to stay ahead. *Yes!* The gray son of Just Victory was slowly falling back. Champion was too much for him!

"Griffen has nowhere to go between horses," the announcer called. "But wait! Limitless Time attacks on the outside. Griffen is asking her colt for speed. . . ."

Cindy looked quickly over her shoulder. Limitless Time was roaring down the track. In seconds he was up with them—Limitless had taken the lead by half a length with only two furlongs to the wire!

Champion was tiring. Cindy could feel it in his labored strides, and his neck was blackened with sweat. But he was barely gaining on Limitless. The brush with Chivalrous Knight had taken a lot out of him—maybe too much for him to win!

"They're down to the final furlong in a furious stretch duel," the announcer shouted. "It's still Limitless Time by a neck!"

"Come on, Champion," Cindy cried. She pressed her body forward, tightening her hands against his neck. With every bit of will she had, Cindy concentrated on telling Champion that she needed more from him. "Do it for me!" she whispered.

Champion found another gear! The sand was slowing him, but he was gaining on Limitless . . . he was drawing clear! Cindy was so close to Ashleigh, she could have easily touched the other jockey.

"And it's Wonder's Champion, headed for home!" the announcer cried. "He's fighting harder than he ever did in his life! But can he do it. . . . Yes, ladies and gentlemen! Champion wins it by one. We have a Horse of the World!"

"Oh, Champion!" Cindy galloped out the colt another furlong, then slowed him to a trot. She leaned forward to hug him around the neck. Cindy vaguely heard the roar of the crowd and the announcer's shouts, but her thoughts were only of the valiant colt who had given her and the race his all.

The floodlights burst into a rainbow of color as Cindy's eyes blurred with happy tears. "You *are* the greatest horse in the world!" she whispered.

Champion proudly arched his neck and shook his head, as if to acknowledge her words. At a slow, high-stepping trot he paraded back to the gap.

"What a ride, sweetheart!" Ian was beside her, smiling hugely.

"Thanks, Dad." Cindy wiped her eyes and tried to compose herself.

"Are you coming?" Ashleigh was beside her on Limitless, as close as she had been in the race. "The racing officials want us both up on the podium to receive the trophy."

Cindy turned to Ashleigh with a worried frown. *How does Ashleigh feel about losing?* she wondered.

Ashleigh smiled. "I think the best horse won."

Cindy smiled broadly back. "If you'd ridden Champion, he would have won, too," she said seriously.

"I don't know, Cindy." Ashleigh shook her head. "He's a great horse, but you two have always had a special bond. He gave everything he had for you tonight. But I'm satisfied with the outcome of the race. I wanted Limitless to have his chance, and he did—he ran a fine race."

"Let's get some pictures!" called a photographer.

"Shall we?" Ashleigh asked. She and Cindy dismounted. Linking arms, they stepped back onto the track with their horses.

Nothing could be more wonderful than this, Cindy thought happily as flashbulbs dazzled her eyes. *Champion and I showed the whole world tonight that he's the best Thoroughbred racehorse and a true descendant of the noble Arabians. And we showed everyone that we're a team, on top of the world.*

JOANNA CAMPBELL was born and raised in Norwalk, Connecticut, and grew up loving horses. She eventually owned a horse of her own and took riding lessons for a number of years, specializing in jumping. She still rides when possible and has started her three-year-old granddaughter on lessons. In addition to publishing over twenty-five novels for young adults, she is the author of four adult novels. She has also sung and played piano professionally and owned an antique business. She now lives on the coast of Maine in Camden with her husband, Ian Bruce. She has two childern, Kimberly and Kenneth, and three grandchildren.

KAREN BENTLEY rode in English equitation and jumping classes as a child and in Western equitation and barrelracing classes as a teenager. She has bred and raised Quarter Horses and, during a sojourn on the East Coast, owned a half-Thoroughbred jumper. She now owns a red roan registered Quarter Horse with some reining moves and lives in New Mexico. She has published nine novels for young adults.